I0608726

HENRIETTE DELILLE

A Servant of Slaves

OTHER WORKS
BY THE AUTHOR

Fiction

Gemini (1959)

The God Hunters (1964)

The Tyree Legend (1979)

Witness (1985)

The Sweet Summer (2000)

Nonfiction

Miracle in the Evening (1960)
The Autobiography of Norman Bel Geddes
(edited by William Kelley)

Film

Witness (1986)
(Winner of the Academy Award for Best Screenplay)

The Blue Lightning (1986)

HENRIETTE DELILLE

A Servant of Slaves

A HISTORICAL NOVEL

William Kelley

A Crossroad Book
The Crossroad Publishing Company
New York

The Crossroad Publishing Company
www.crossroadpublishing.com

Copyright © 2003 by William Kelley

All rights reserved. No part of this book may be reproduced, stored in a retrieval system, or transmitted, in any form or by any means, electronic, mechanical, photocopying, recording, or otherwise, without the written permission of The Crossroad Publishing Company. For permissions, please email rights@crossroadpublishing.com

Printed in the United States of America

Cataloging-in-Publication Data is available from the Library of Congress

ISBN (13-digit) 978-0-8245-2216-2

Books published by The Crossroad Publishing Company may be purchased at special quantity discount rates for classes and institutional use. For information, please email sales@crossroadpublishing.com.

For Dorris Halsey,
my beloved agent, who early on predicted
that the publication of this book would constitute
Henriette Delille's third miracle.
With all my love.

Contents

Acknowledgments

I want to acknowledge, above all, the assistance and advice of Roy Carlisle — a fine man, a good friend, and a superlative editor. The following books have been of special help:

Sacred Arts of Haitian Vodou, edited by Donald J. Cosentino.

No Cross, No Crown: Black Nuns in Nineteenth-Century New Orleans, by Sister Mary Bernard Deggs, edited by Virgina Meacham Gould and Charles E. Nolan.

Creole New Orleans: Race and Americanization, edited by Arnold R. Hirsch and Joseph Logsdon.

End of an Era: New Orleans, 1850 to 1860, by Robert C. Reinders. The menu on p. 37 is taken from this book.

Finally, I would like to express my entire appreciation to Charles E. Nolan, archivist of the Archdiocese of New Orleans, who allowed me total access to all of the papers and documents relating to the lives of Henriette Delille and Etienne Rousselon. Any essential error of fact in this novel can in no way be laid at the feet of Mr. Nolan, who as an archivist and a gentleman has no peer.

Prologue

Last Monday there died one of those women whose obscure and retired life has nothing remarkable in the eyes of the world, but is full of merit before God. Miss Henriette Delille had for long years consecrated herself totally to God without reservation to the instruction of the ignorant and principally to the slave. To perpetuate this kind of apostolate, so different yet so necessary, she had founded with the help of certain pious persons the House of the Holy Family, a house poor and little known except by the poor and the young, and which for the past ten or twelve years has produced, quietly, a considerable good which will continue. Having never heard of philanthropy, this poor maid has done more than the great philanthropists with their systems so brilliant yet so vain. Worn out by work, she died at the age of fifty years after a long and painful illness borne with the most edifying resignation. The crowd gathered for her funeral testified by its sorrow how keenly felt was the loss of her who for the love of Jesus Christ had made herself the humble servant of slaves.

— New Orleans Tribune

PART ONE

1836–1837

❧ HENRIETTE ❧

ONE

Now, in late October, the wharves were filling with steamboats from upriver and the Gulf Coast, flatboats from all over the vast Mississippi drainage, and ships from every coast and country in the world. All along the thin crescent quay, the clatter and clamor, the catcalls, bawling, and curses of the men — the Negroes, the Irish, the Gascons, the Spanish, the Yankees, the Italians, the Portagees, and Cajuns and Creoles — shattered the adjacent air and, carried on the soft breezes of that Saturday afternoon, gave notice to the entire French Quarter that commerce was boisterously alive and sweating in the Port of New Orleans.

As the two women turned off Dauphine onto Toulouse and headed toward the river, the noise from the levee came clear and harsh. Betsy stopped short. "Oh, Lordy God, Miss Henriette, listen to that. Every sailor and dockhand in the city is drunk. Listen to them. I told you Saturday afternoon ain't no time to go visiting along the wharf."

"We're not going to the wharf."

"Well, next thing to it, from Bourbon Street on. And it just ain't right for a young lady."

"Nonsense, Betsy. Now come along. I don't want to be late."

"Oh, we be late, all right," said Betsy, beginning to move again. "The late Miss Delille and her maid, Betsy Bushrod. Late and daid from getting their throats cut."

"We're in God's hands."

"*You* in God's hands. I ain't even under his fingernail."

"Don't you talk like that. You've been baptized."

"Well, they say you cain't baptize a slave. It just don't take."

15

"*They* don't know what they're talking about," Henriette said, somewhat sharply. "Now get up here and walk beside me like a proper Creole."

"Yes, ma'am."

As they crossed Bourbon Street and continued along Toulouse, a swarthy flatboatman with a big broad-brimmed leather hat came backing out of a saloon door, dragging a tall woman behind him. He was facing her, both hands at her throat, shouting, "Come easy, or I drag you!"

The woman grabbed the saloon door with one hand and struck at the flatboatman with the other. "You crazy man, let me go!" she screamed, and swung her right fist again. This time she landed the punch, and the flatboatman staggered backward and fell into the gutter. The woman darted back into the saloon. The flatboatman got to his feet, stood swaying for a moment, and then turned, grinned his nearly toothless grin at the spectators, and shouted, "I am, by God, going to find me a woman to ball by nightfall, or my names ain't Billy and Milo Sweeney!" He glowered around and spotted Henriette, stopped in the middle of Bourbon Street, Betsy beside her.

"There!" he said. "There stands a fine-looking white woman with her darky! She's a no-doubt, by-God virgin, and of entire use to nobody!" He then waved both hands in the air, fell flat on his face, and began to cough up blood.

Henriette had already started to move toward the man when Betsy grabbed her near arm with both hands. "Don't you dare!" she said fiercely. "Don't you ever dare!"

"But the poor man is bleeding," Henriette said.

"That ain't blood! That just busthead whiskey!" Betsy said.

"But it's red."

"They makes it red!" Betsy said, pushing her toward the other side of the street. "And you ain't going to disgrace yourself trying to plug him up! Move on, now! Move!"

They were crossing Royal Street before Henriette spoke. "I know you mean well, Betsy, but you were wrong. Please don't do that again."

"Bite your tongue!" Betsy said sharply. "I'll do it again! I'll do it ever' damn time!"

When they arrived at St. Claude Street School, Betsy saw her to the door but refused to come inside.

"Why won't you come in?" Henriette said.

"Cause I don't like 'em," Betsy said. "I don't like anybody's going to take you away from me." And Betsy turned away, but not before Henriette saw the tears standing in her eyes.

She knelt at the back of the small chapel listening to the sweet, lilting chant of the nuns as they sang the Office of St. Mary for Saturday. She held her eyes closed, absorbing the sound and soul of it, and praying under it with a fervid passion that made her shudder.

Oh, Lord I am not worthy. But take the stiffness from their necks and persuade them. Fill them with charity and the good grace to accept me into their holy company.

The nuns, seated, now moved forward to their knees to begin the hymn for vespers.

> Ave maris stella
> Dei Mater alma
> Atque semper Virgo,
> Felix caeli porta.

The nuns sat back after the first verse and continued the stately hymn. Henriette knelt motionless, allowing the words to flow over her, tempering, softening the anxiety that overwhelmed her. She prayed: *Holy Mother, I am truly not worthy. I know this. But I pray that you will indulge me. I pray that you will take my body, my spirit, my heart, and my soul, and impose them upon this sacred congregation. Make them want me, dear Mother. Make them see past my skin and my blood. Make them see my soul and smile upon me.*

The nuns were almost finished with the *Sancrosancte* before Henriette came fully to herself. She managed to get to her feet, gather her things, quickstep toward the front of the chapel, and arrive before the portress — regarding her with imperious eye — could pull the heavy iron cloister gate shut.

"Please," Henriette said.

The nun regarded her coldly, looking her up and down. "Surely, you are not for the kitchen," she said.

"No," Henriette said. "I am to see Mother Superior."

"Oh," the nun said sourly, "You are the new teacher."

"No," Henriette said. "I am the new postulant."

And she strode through the half-open gate, her skirts rustling, praying: *God give me the strength to be meek and humble, to become the least daughter of this house.*

But when she heard the gate clang shut behind her, she flinched and felt herself begin to tremble.

Mother Catherine smiled thinly at her across the parlor. A spare, regal woman with austere features, the mother superior held her chin high, giving her face the sharpness of a cutting stone. She adjusted her pince-nez to one of her brilliant blue eyes, picked up a paper from her lap, glanced at it for a moment, and then fixed her gaze on Henriette.

"So, Miss Delille, we meet again."

"Yes, Mother. Thank you for making time for me."

"Well, you're very welcome, my dear. Just what is it I can do for you? Your letter is quite vague on the point."

Henriette felt a shiver along her spine. This was not going to be easy. "I have come to renew my petition for admission to the Ursuline Order."

Mother Catherine stared at her for a moment, then looked away, heaving a long sigh. "I thought we had resolved this matter with some finality."

"Yes, Mother."

"You are a quadroon?"

"Yes, Mother."

"And you know that the Order does not admit women of color."

"Yes, Mother."

"Then what on earth is there to discuss?"

Henriette stared down at her white gloves, silently called upon St. Teresa to stand by her, and then lifted her eyes to Mother Catherine's. "I thought," she said, her voice anguished and small, "that if I saw you face to face after these several years and you could see how fervently I still wish to be a nun...if I told you personally that I would be willing to do the lowliest tasks — clean, and wash, and cherish the dying and the dead, especially our poor slaves — that I would never complain or hesitate or shirk my assigned duties for the rest of my life...if I told you this and you saw that I meant it with all my heart, then...then, I hoped, you might relent."

Mother Catherine looked at her with a small frown. "It is not a question of my relenting. But you have made a quite extraordinary statement. You are a very handsome girl of obvious privilege and education. What would you know about the dying and the dead? The filth and stench and despair of the death of slaves? What could you possibly know?"

"I know a little, because I have tended them. Some few of them."

"And how have you done this?"

"With the help of Juliette and Josephine, my dear friends. We have taken female slaves from the streets where they lay dying.

We carried them to a vacant barn that we know of, and cared for them, and taught them about Jesus, and even baptized them at the time of death. Then we would get Charles, who is a slave who has the use of a horse and wagon, and take the bodies to Potter's Field and bury them." Henriette paused and then hastened to add, "Potter's Field is consecrated ground, of course."

Mother Catherine stared at her, her lips moving but no words coming forth. "I am astonished. You did these things without calling for a priest?"

"We always asked for a priest, but none would come. They are so busy."

Mother Catherine was still staring. "My child, you overwhelm me. What on earth would possess you? I mean, I would not ask even my own nuns...." Her voice fell away. "God love you."

"And God love you, Mother." Henriette got to her feet. "I am sorry to have troubled you."

Mother Catherine looked at her, tears starting in her eyes. "Troubled me? You have edified me." She got to her feet. "I wish with all my heart I could receive you as a postulant in this order. But, God forgive me, I cannot."

"Don't be upset, Mother. I should not have presumed. God bless you." Henriette curtsied, turned quickly, crossed to the parlor door, and went out.

Mother Catherine sat down, blinking as the door closed behind Henriette. "And God bless you, child." Then, very quietly, she said, "Dear God, I am not worthy."

She left the school through the chapel. She knelt at the altar rail, looked for a moment at the tabernacle, and then slowly leaned forward and put her forehead to the cold marble of the rail and softly spoke her prayer. "I believe in God. I hope in God. I love. I wish to live and die for God."

She held her head against the stone for some moments and then blessed herself, got to her feet, and walked — bent at the shoulders — out to where Betsy waited.

"I'm sorry to keep you waiting, Betsy."

"Never mind. What'd they say?"

"Mother Catherine was very nice."

"But what'd she say?"

"She said no, Betsy."

"Well," Betsy said, "she's as big a damned fool as the rest of them." Hurrying to catch up with Henriette, she said, "But God keep her stone-cold heart."

"Betsy," Henriette said, "bite your tongue."

TWO

The Delille home on Burgundy Street had been purchased by Henriette's mother, Maria Diaz, in 1805. It was painted, fittingly enough, in subdued burgundy with white trim and had black wrought-iron scrollwork at the windows and balcony railings on all three stories. Her two daughters, Cecile and Henriette Delille, still lived there, along with Cecile's four children. The children were the issue of a formal alliance between Cecile and a wealthy Austrian businessman by the name of Samuel Hart, who lived in the house next door. This alliance was typical of the arrangements entered into by hundreds of quadroon girls at the time, an option that was certainly open to Henriette who, at twenty-four, was an extraordinary beauty.

She sat now in her room at the top of the house reading a French Rule of St. Augustine. She was a bit puzzled by Augustine's concentration in chapters 6 and 7 on the subject of custody of the eyes. She read aloud the quotation from Proverbs 28:20: "An abomination to the Lord is he that fixeth his gaze."

What's this? she thought. Anyone who seriously pursues a life in Jesus Christ knows she must control her eyes. It should be second nature by the time she is twelve years of age. And when the great man went on to say, "And let what I have said about not fixing one's gaze be observed also in regard to other disorders: to find them out, to prevent them, to make them known, to prove and punish them carefully and in accordance with the truth, with hatred for sin and love for the brother man!"

Henriette again spoke aloud. "Well, of course," she said. "And then gently ease her out of your midst." She closed the book and looked at the wall. "Am I being too harsh? I don't think so. This foolishness of the eyes cannot be tolerated. There should be no such nonsense, no least shadow of turning."

There was a soft knock at the door, which was almost immediately opened by Cecile. "Well," she said, smiling, "I've caught you talking to yourself again."

Henriette returned her smile. "I was having a word with St. Augustine."

"You do keep good company."

"You have spoiled me."

"I'm hardly a saint."

"I'll be the judge of that. Won't you sit down?"

Cecile took a chair by the window. "I was talking with Betsy."

"Oh?"

"She told me about the Ursulines. Mother Catherine was very nice."

"But she said no."

"Yes, she did. I was not surprised, really."

"I wish I could say I was sorry."

"I wouldn't believe you if you did." Henriette smiled. "I know how you feel."

"Oh, Henriette, I don't mean to be cruel. But you are so stubborn. Someone has to point these things out to you."

"No. I'm quite well aware of the cost of my persistence." Her voice trailed off. "I accept it all as God's will for me."

"But how can you be so sure that he wills you to be a religious? Especially when you have refused to give anything else a chance?"

"Anything else doesn't interest me." She smiled. "Cecile, I know you mean well, but I am not interested in marriage, or in any other sort of . . . liaison."

"Of course you aren't. And you won't be. Until you meet the right man."

"Cecile —"

"And you will never meet him as long as you insist upon hiding yourself away. We're having the first of the grand opera balls at the Orleans Theater in two weeks, and I —"

"No, no."

"You could go as my attendant. But at least you'd be seen."

"I don't want to be 'seen.'"

"Henriette, you are a single woman with absolutely no prospects. You want to be a nun, but they won't have you. You will soon be too old for any arrangement. Are you simply determined to be a spinster?"

Henriette waited a long moment. "I am determined to be a bride of Jesus Christ. And I will be."

"How will you do that if no order will have you? Can't you see that you are at a dead end?"

"Am I a burden to you?"

"No, no, of course not." Cecile looked at her, blinking. "Oh, Henriette, please don't misunderstand. I love you. I just want what is best for you."

"I know, dear Cecile. I know what is best for me. Trust me to find my way."

Cecile sat for a moment, looking at her. Then she got to her feet. "I have presumed, and I am sorry."

Henriette rose, crossed to her, and put her arms around her. "You are only trying to help, and I love you for it."

Cecile turned, went to the door, and looked back impishly. "But the opera ball will be especially lavish this year." And she went out.

Henriette smiled after her. "And may God be especially merciful," she said quietly. "And keep us all in his grace."

THREE

They had been talking for more than an hour, covering ground they had covered many times before, but now with a special intensity. Juliette Gaudin took notes and looked up as Henriette stopped in midsentence and slapped both hands down on her thighs.

"Enough talk," she said. "It is time to stop talking and to declare ourselves."

Josephine Charles smiled and nodded. "Oh, I like that, Henriette," she said. "We'll have a broadside printed, and we'll distribute it around the city."

"No, no. Nothing so public," Henriette said. "We will simply declare ourselves to one another, in a formal document that may be shown later when there are those who wish to join us."

"Just so," said Juliette. "And are we decided what we should call ourselves."

"Why, yes," Henriette said. "As you suggested earlier."

Juliette nodded, shuffled her papers, found one, and read aloud from it. "The Congregation of the Sisters of the Presentation of the Blessed Virgin Mary."

"Oh, love it," Josephine said. "It sounds so . . . official."

"It is official," Henriette said. "It is a sodality, and we are the officers."

"But you are the foundress," Juliette Gaudin said softly. "There is no question about that."

"Well," Henriette said, "I thought that perhaps all three of us — "

"No," Juliette said, interrupting. "We must make it clear for those who come after. You brought us together; you hold us together. It is as it is." She dipped her pen in the inkwell and went back to her writing.

Juliette Gaudin was four years older than Henriette and, like Henriette and Josephine and Juliette's mother before her, was a free woman of color. She was born in Cuba after her family had fled the revolution in Saint-Domingue and had been brought to New Orleans when the Cubans expelled the Saint-Domingue refugees. She was Henriette's closest and staunchest friend and brooked no nonsense — least of all from Henriette — as to who was in charge.

Josephine Charles had been born in New Orleans of a German father and a quadroon mother. She was tall, stately, beautiful, and had been much courted. She had, like Henriette, an aristocratic bearing, a nearly white complexion, and an imperiously self-possessed gaze. Her sense of humor was a bit sharp, but her devotion to Henriette and "the work" was absolute.

Josephine now smiled and looked around at Henriette. "Well, do we now call ourselves sisters?"

"Why, I think so," Henriette said. "We're not an order, to be sure, not yet, but we are certainly sisters in our devotions to one another and to our common purpose."

"We are sisters," said Juliette Gaudin, still writing furiously. "Who is to say we are not?"

"The bishop might object," said Josephine.

"The bishop will probably never know we exist," said Henriette. "But if and when he does discover us, I will discuss the matter with him."

"Bishop Blanc is a good man," Josephine said. "He'll support us."

Henriette got to her feet. "Well," she said, "whether they like us or not, we are set upon our course. And we will stay the course, and we will make our mark."

The other two stood up, and the ladies embraced. And Josephine Charles said, "St. Paul would be proud."

"It is as it is," said Juliette.

❧ ETIENNE ❧

FOUR

There was a sound like the bark of a small dog. I looked up from my breviary and turned toward the door. Bishop Antoine Blanc stood there, his cupped hand to his mouth, looking embarrassed.

"I beg your pardon, Father Rousselon. Too many onions at lunch."

"Come in, Bishop," I said, getting to my feet. "How was your trip?"

"Abominable. Getting to Baton Rouge and back is one definition of eternity." He came in, took the chair I offered him, and heaved a great sigh. "I'm sorry I wasn't here to greet you, Father. How was the boat trip?"

"Another definition of eternity," I said, sitting down.

"I've interrupted your office?" he said, glancing at the book in my right hand.

"No, no. Just an Office of the Dead."

He heaved another sigh, this one with a whistle in it. "Oh, Lord. So many old friends. So many dead. I'm woefully behind in my dead offices.

"Bishops are required to say them?"

"Of course. One remains a priest." He sniffed at the air. "God, it's hot. Don't be in a rush to become a bishop. It is merely priestly exhaustion raised to the second power."

"I harbor no such ambition."

"Good. Now tell me, how is France? Is it still there?"

"It was when I left."

"And dear Lyon?"

"Thriving."

27

"And the restaurants?"

"I'm afraid I hadn't much time for restaurants. They kept me very busy at the seminary."

"Of course. We have some first-rate restaurants here. Moreau's, the St. Charles Hotel, Victor's...we'll catch you up on fine dining." He glanced up at me. "If you are at all interested."

"Well, one does have to eat." I smiled, and he seemed reassured.

"Splendid." He glanced about the room. I had unpacked my traveling bags and put things away, but my trunk — a large, metal-strapped, coffin-shaped parting gift of the seminary faculty, just delivered by three grunting draymen — stood against one wall, its lid up. And on top, sticking out of a sock I had packed it in, was a bottle of Hennessy cognac, given to me by my senior students. I saw the bishop's eye light upon it, move away, and then dart back. And, suddenly, God's grace moved me to do the right thing.

I jumped to my feet. "Bishop," I said, "may I offer you a drink?"

"Why, certainly, Father. You mean that you brought something with you?"

"As a matter of fact, thanks to my students, I did."

"Well, then."

"And two snifter glasses in which to serve it."

"Cognac?"

"The best, I believe." I walked over, took the bottle out of its sock, and handed it to the bishop. He handled it like a chalice.

"Dear Lord. Hennessy three-star. V.O." he said reverently.

I took the two glasses out of the other sock and set them on the side table next to his chair. I found my corkscrew and handed it to the bishop. "If you'd like," I said.

"My distinct honor," he said. He opened the bottle quite expertly, poured both glasses a quarter full, and handed me one. "Father, I give you New Orleans and the success of your mission here."

"With all my heart," I said. He smiled. We touched glasses and sipped. I have never much liked brandy and this, while quite smooth, was overpowering. I took a deep breath. The bishop looked up at me, eyes glowing.

"My liver may snarl at me, but this is delicious. Your students have excellent taste."

"One of them is a Hennessy," I said. "Richard Hennessy."

"Studying for the priesthood?"

"No. Just very interested in theology."

"Why not? Theology and cognac both require exquisite taste, and both are eminently perfectible. I give you Mr. Hennessy."

We clicked glasses and drank again. This time it was a little easier. "To Richard," I said. "And to my bishop."

"Please call me Antoine," he said. "I've not been a bishop that long."

"And please call me Etienne."

"Well, I will begin, Etienne, by offering you an apology. It is my fault you are here, you know."

"I beg your pardon?"

"I wasn't going to admit this, but I've had my eye on you since you became dean at the seminary. And when it appeared that you were about to be promoted to rector, I struck. I sent an urgent request to Bishop Foucault, who is an old friend, and the deed was done." He looked at me quite seriously. "I hope you can forgive me."

"There is nothing to forgive, Antoine. I was ready for an adventure, a spiritual challenge, and you have given it to me."

"You are too generous."

"Merely honest."

"You like New Orleans?"

"I didn't say that."

We both laughed. "It grows on you," he said.

"I'm sure it will."

"Which brings us nicely round to what I have in mind for your first assignment."

I reached for the bottle and poured us both another drink. "I am eager to hear it," I said.

"Understand, first, that I anticipate making you my chief administrative assistant. The vicar-general of the diocese."

"Antoine, I — " I was quite frankly floored by his directness, but before I could continue, he interrupted. "Within the year. But in order to get you involved in the business of the diocese, I am going to appoint you chaplain to the Ursuline school up on St. Claude Street. Anyone who needs breaking in will certainly get it from the Ursulines."

I nodded. "They are formidable women."

"Especially Mother Catherine. She could mount a crusade." He set his glass down and gestured that he'd had enough. "They run two schools, actually. One for white girls, and one for the daughters of free people of color. They also do what they can to instruct the slave children."

"There are no schools for the slaves?"

"I'm afraid not, Etienne. There are two or three devout women who do what they can. You'll meet them. They use the school class-rooms after school hours." He stood up. "I'll walk you up there tomorrow. It's about six blocks north. Introduce you, all that."

"Am I to continue living here?" I asked, getting to my feet.

"Of course." He looked around. "I'm sure we can find you a better room." He turned to go. "That was delicious. Thank you very much."

I took his hand and started to kneel to kiss his ring. But he pulled me up, smiling. "Plenty of time for that. God bless you, Etienne, and welcome."

"Thank you, Antoine."

"Sleep well. Goodnight."

He went out briskly, nodding at me from the door. I hesitated, poured myself another small drink, sat down, and looked up at the crucifix on the wall. And so it begins, dear God. Give me the strength and the courage. And help me to lose my fear of nuns.

FIVE

Thursday

Where we are living is the Old Ursuline Convent on Chartres Street, a magnificent old pile of cypress planks built in 1753. I don't know the dimensions of the building, but I believe you could park two steamboats end to end in it and still have room for a bargeful of belted Galloways.

The old building has seen its share of history. The great fire of 1788 burned the Church of St. Louis and many houses, but a bucket brigade of Negroes saved the convent, the Royal Hospital, and the nearby barracks. The convent served as a sort of spiritual headquarters during the great Battle of New Orleans in 1815. Add to that the heroics of the Ursuline nuns who suffered frigid winters and torrid summers within these walls for almost a hundred years, and you have a very impressive past.

Yesterday, just after I arrived—and only one of the nuns was here to greet me—I made a bold exploration of the convent from top to bottom. I climbed the broad wooden stairs to the second floor, found what appeared to be the bishop's office, and pressed on down the hall, thinking that this must have been where the nuns had lived. I was right. There were rows of cells on either side, numbers on their great wooden doors. I walked down the long corridor to about the middle and then pushed into one of the cells.

There were single bunks on either side, both built of cypress planks, both covered by the thinnest straw mats I have ever seen. One of the bunks had a chamber pot under it, and the other had under it what appeared to be a leather cat-o'-nine tails. The window between the bunks was about a foot square, its panes, translucent at best, yellow in the bright sun. It was unopenable. It was a hot day, but not very hot. Still, the air in the cell was so oppressive, so heavy with dust, that I found it difficult to breathe and felt sweat running down my back and face.

31

I turned to go, but then turned back and knelt at the foot of one of the bunks. I prayed, "Dear sisters who lived in this cell, I give you the joy of Jesus. I marvel at your strength and endurance. This cell must have been purgatory most of the time. I hope you persevered. I hope you are somewhere happy in Christ. Amen."

Which was very sentimental of me, I'm sure, but I have a particular affection for nuns. I'm somewhat afraid of them, as I've mentioned. It is their fierceness, their total dedication that frightens me, that leaves me in awe. But in a way I love them too, just as I fear and love God.

Antoine and I walked up to St. Claude Street School in mid-afternoon in a steady drizzle, and it was a revelation. I hadn't seen much of the city before this, having been met virtually at the gang-plank and whisked off to the Old Convent in the bishop's trap. It had been raining and the window flaps were secured, so I hadn't been able to see much until I was delivered into the school court-yard. But my nose had been working perfectly, and I had smelled some very horrendous smells like ordure and rotting flesh and, for one moment, was convinced I was in the middle of a pig sty full of decomposing animals. I nearly gagged and wondered what in the name of God could produce such a calamitous odor in the middle of a civilized municipality.

I found out on our walk to the school.

To begin, there are few paved or bricked or even wooden public sidewalks. One walks in a soupy quagmire on either side of most streets. Antoine, who apologized for the conditions and for not using his trap (he didn't like to on short distances, saying he needed the exercise) said that he had done his best to interest local government in building some sidewalks but got nowhere. He did think that slosh-ing along with everybody else was probably good for one's humility. But it was very hard on one's shoes and the skirts of one's soutane. Not to mention (I thought, but didn't say) the preservation of one's ankles from putrefaction.

In the course of the seven-block walk, I counted four dead dogs, two dead cats, two dead cows, a huge dead goat, and one dead horse, all decomposing in the streets. I kept glancing at Antoine for some sign of dismay or revulsion, but he is apparently inured to it all—a state to which I devoutly pray to God I never attain.

As we turned toward Bayou Road and toward the swamp beyond, we were assailed by a breeze full of the most noxious, mephitic air I have ever had to inhale.

"Good Lord," I said. "What on earth?"

"The swamp," Antoine said. "Gormley's Basin is the worst of it."

He then went on to explain what caused this dreadful stink, but I wasn't hearing very well. Later I came upon an account by a British medical writer who summed it up nicely.

> The appearance of the hot sun, after a rain, speedily covers (Gormley's Basin) with a deep green mantle which, in a few hours of solar action, converts into an elevated black foam. As the evaporation goes on, nearly the whole space becomes uncovered.... The basin yields up its dead, and the whole necropolis of departed animal and vegetable life lies naked to the rays of the sun. To crown it all, the whole district is occupied by a series of soap factories and tanneries which no precaution can prevent from exhaling an offensive odor.

An offensive odor? If smells could kill, I would have dropped dead on the spot! I determined to find out exactly where Gormley's Basin was located and to avoid ever getting within a mile of it.

By the time we got to the school, I was ill at the stomach. But I swallowed my gorge and persevered. School was out for the day, but Mother Catherine had arranged to meet us in the parlor. She sat very straight, almost haughtily, in her parlor chair, reminding me of a sergeant of grenadiers. She figured me out immediately.

"You look sick," she said.

"It is not serious," I said.

"Mother, this is Father Etienne Rousselon. He has just arrived. Father, this is Mother Catherine," Antoine said, bowing.

"I am very pleased to meet you," I said.

"You look sick, Reverend Father."

"A temporary indisposition," I said.

"No, I don't think so," she said.

"I assure you—"

"He looks like he's about to vomit," she said.

"No, no," Antoine said. "Father, why don't you take a look around." He smiled at Mother Catherine. "He's going to be your new chaplain."

"God help us," Mother Catherine said, and she was still clucking and peering at me as the bishop led her away toward the chapel.

I was dismayed. Nuns have always been able to dismay me. It is as if certain of them can see into my soul and perceive the wretched state of my resolve and intentions. It is an uncanny business, and of all those who have had me plumbed and pilloried at first glance, Mother Catherine ranked right up there with my own aunt, who was a Benedictine abbess. At that moment, I looked forward to my chaplaincy as I might toward a long tour of purgatory.

There were three classrooms, which were small, dismal rooms containing one table and maybe a dozen straight chairs with a rough-hewn cross nailed over the door. I was about to turn away before I got to the third classroom when I heard a soft, urgent, female voice coming from inside the room.

"Jesus died on the cross for you," the voice said.

I moved up to the open door and looked in. There was a young woman, who appeared to be white, talking to two very black little girls. The young lady's voice was cultivated, soft, self-assured, and she was quite comely—a beauty in fact—and, as she became aware of my presence and turned to look at me, startled me with the intensity of her eyes.

"Good afternoon, Father. May I help you?"

"Good afternoon." I stayed at the door. "I'm sorry to interrupt. Please go on."

"We're finished for the day. You may go now, girls. I will see you here next week."

"Yes'm," they said in unison, and they walked to the door and eased past me, looking up, their eyes big as teacups.

"My name is Henriette Delille," the young woman said.

"I am Father Etienne Rousselon. I've only just arrived. I am to be your new chaplain."

"Why that's splendid," she said. "The sisters will be very pleased."

"You are not an Ursuline?"

"No, I am a quadroon. I am not eligible."

"I see. And they make no exceptions?"

"None of the congregations do."

"But you do teach here?"

"No. Not formally. The sisters just let me use the classroom. For the little slave girls."

"They are slaves, those little ones?"

"Yes. And there is no one else for them."

"Not even the sisters?"

"They do what they can. But they don't go to places like Congo Square, where I found those two little ones."

"Congo Square?"

"The slave market. One of them."

I shook my head. "That's hard to imagine."

"You don't have to imagine, Father. It is a short walk west of here."

"I meant the whole business of slavery."

"Well, in New Orleans, it is a fact of life."

"Yes. Well, I hope I am able to help you in your work, Miss Delille."

"Oh, you will be of great help. There will be any number of baptisms. And last rites and funerals. Oh, my yes. We will keep you very, very busy."

I smiled at her enthusiasm, and she smiled back. "I look forward to it."

"Thank you, Father." She suddenly fell to her knees. "May I have your blessing?"

I placed my hand on her head very briefly and spoke the words of the blessing much too quickly. She didn't seem to notice but took my hand, kissed it, and got to her feet looking radiant.

"God bless you, Father, and welcome" she said. "I must go now."

She bowed her head and moved past me, going quickstep down the corridor. I stood looking after her — her regal carriage, her threadbare black dress — and found myself thinking that I had just met a very remarkable person.

SIX

Monday

When I got back to my room, I found a note from the bishop, who had made his separate way back. "My dear Etienne. I realize that this day has been something of a shock to you. By way of making up for it and by way of welcoming you to New Orleans, I would be honored to host a dinner for both of us at the St. Charles Hotel. The trap will be ready in the courtyard at 8:00 p.m. In his name, Antoine."

I sat down on the bed, looked down at my filthy shoes and the mud-caked skirts of my soutane, and, after a moment, I smiled. God certainly had an unpredictable sense of humor. I had arrived back at the Great Convent ready to lie down and weep. And now, faced with a festive evening, I would have to smile. Even laugh. I wasn't sure I could bring it off. I was certainly hungry — the convent fare I'd sampled at breakfast was spartan, to say the least — but could I really sit down to a feast in this stinkpot of a city? In this place of rot and desperation and the pitiful starving poor?

Yes, of course I could. Because it pleased my bishop. And perhaps he was right. Even Christ went to a banquet now and then. Right. Go along, Rousselon, and have a good time. Just don't forget to take your cross with you.

The St. Charles Hotel was nearly new, having been built in 1835. It was an enormous square of marble four stories high with six frontal pillars, room for a thousand guests, and a dining room that could seat four hundred at a time. The seating was at three long tables in a room decorated with five massive chandeliers and offering silver service for every diner. The food, the menu assured, was prepared by a chef from Paris, and the menu itself was a double broadside listing ten courses from soup to dessert.

The bishop was received with great deference, and we were seated at the middle table. Antoine ordered a modest Bordeaux and we were faced with the menu. Now, I had been to a fine restaurant or two in Lyon, but I have never seen anything like the largesse of this bill of fare. Let me try to give some small notion.

The soups were ox-joint and vermicelli.

The fish was baked red snapper with oyster sauce.

The boiled course was corned beef, sugar-cured ham, and leg of mutton with caper sauce.

The roast meats: beef, loin of lamb, pig with apple sauce, loin of pork, loin of mutton, and loin of veal.

The entrees: beef à la mode, calf's head with brain sauce, croquettes of rice with lemon sauce, calf's feet à la Pascaline, veal and ham scalloped with mushrooms, macaroni with Italian sauce, and oyster patties.

The vegetables: Irish potatoes, hominy, rice, beans, spinach, and cabbage.

Condiments: Worcestershire sauce, walnut and tomato catsup, Cumberland sauce, Harvey sauce, John Bull sauce, and mixed pickles.

Pastries and puddings included gooseberry pie, Pethivier pie, Genoese perlies, biscuits Milanais, anisette jelly, and English creams. And, almost finally, there were raisins, filberts, almonds, and pecans.

I say almost finally because Antoine chose to end the meal with vintage port, Cuban cigars, and chicory coffee. Exactly what I had to eat is not important. After dessert, I remember being stuffed.

After the port and cigar, I remember being glassy-eyed, which made things look fat, out of focus, and Antoine himself to appear huge, especially around the jowls. It wasn't that I had gorged myself: I simply was not used to such an excessive quantity of food and an implied obligation to do my part. My wine glass was kept constantly full (I believe we had three bottles, plus the port), and the waiters kept urging nuts, biscuits, pastries, and creams upon me. In the end, I felt like a distended bladder and fell on my bed at long last praying to Gargantua and Pantagruel (my self-appointed patron saints of gluttony) to intercede for me so that I might live out the night.

But I have neglected our conversation. Antoine had been consecrated bishop of New Orleans on November 22, 1837, so he had been in office a scant year. He had been faced with several immediate problems. The first was the necessity of recruiting clergy from abroad. I was one of the proofs of his success. Second, he needed to establish more parishes in and around New Orleans — an ongoing project. And third was the absolute need to establish a seminary for local vocations, a job he expected to complete within the next two years.

There was one other major problem.

"Rome," he said, "seems to think that Texas and Mexico, in war or peace, are in my easily accessible backyards. A few years ago, there was only one bishop in all of Mexico. And the last I heard, there are only two priests in all of Texas. And they are apparently spiritual disasters. I have told Rome that I have called upon the Vincentians in St. Louis for help and, despite the displeasure of Bishop Rosati of St. Louis, the Vincentians seem eager to undertake the mission, and Rome heartily approves."

I stared at him fascinated. "You are in direct touch with Gregory XVI?"

"Why not, Etienne? He's the pope, and I his humble servant."

"And it's all upon you?"

"Well, there is Bishop Belaunzaran of Monterrey in Mexico. He had Texas under his jurisdiction before the hostilities. He blames the

Texas problem on the Americans because they failed to respond to his request that they send missionaries. I've corresponded with Belaunzaran, but he's retired and not at all amiable."

"Texas is a very large piece of ground."

"So is Mexico. I'm glad I no longer have to worry about both of them. My Vincentians, I feel sure, will take care of Texas."

"Pray God," I said.

He sighed heavily, sipped at his wine, and then suddenly smiled broadly. "But there are bright spots," he said. "I have my vicar-general, my gall bladder has decided to make peace, and the good sisters all over the diocese are doing nobly."

"Thank God for the sisters."

"The true heart of the church."

He raised his glass in an impromptu toast, and I joined him. And, in the moment of silence that followed, I found myself thinking of Henriette Delille. "I met one of the sisters today," I said. "Well, she is not quite a professed sister. A quadroon, actually, who teaches part-time at the Ursuline School. Her name is Delille. Henriette Delille. I was very impressed with her."

The bishop pursed his lips, nodding solemnly. "Yes. A holy woman. A quadroon, to be sure. Poor soul. She is determined to be a nun."

"Can nothing be done to arrange it?"

"Good Lord, no. There would be an outcry you could hear all the way to the Vatican."

"I see."

"I'm glad you do, Etienne. Any least whisper of a person of color joining one of our white female congregations would provoke a mutiny." He chuckled. "An ecclesiastical bloodbath."

We concluded our dinner shortly thereafter, and the matter was not mentioned again. Antoine nodded off as soon as we climbed into the trap, and we rode home in silence. But I included Henriette Delille in my prayers that night, and asked God that she — and all colored persons — should be fully received and empowered in the church of Jesus Christ.

SEVEN

Wednesday

I was awakened the next morning at five by Brother Tobias, who was our valet, butler, chef, and faithful servant. A holy man with a very bad temper.

"Get the hell up," he said at the time of his second *benedicamus Domino*. "Get up or I'll pour cold water on you."

"*Deo gratias*," I said, and fairly leaped to my feet.

I was feeling a bit of resentment over Brother Tobias's rough manners until I saw that he had taken my muddy soutane and cleaned and ironed it. My shoes had been scraped and brightly polished and were sitting atop the folded soutane. I could have kissed the man. The morning chill had taken some of the soupiness out of the mud, but the walk to the St. Claude Street School was nonetheless bizarre. Bars were still doing business, doors wide open to the street, and the music of horns and drums and pianos shattered the brisk morning air, leaving me thinking of the desperation of sin. This was compounded by the voices of the whores who, despite my hat and soutane clearly marking me out as a priest, continually invited me to "have a good time."

"Are you looking for love, little priest?" one asked.

"I am looking for lost souls," I said. She virtually screamed with laughter.

An ancient nun met me at the school and showed me to the chapel. She was Sister Louis, and she kicked a young man awake as we entered the sacristy.

"Up, up, you lazy," she said. Then, to me, "He will serve your Mass. Did you bring some wine?"

"No, Sister. I wasn't told."

"You must learn to think for yourself," she said sharply. "You must make do with what we have. By now it is, of course, vinegar." She looked up at a small pendulum clock on the wall. "Mass in four minutes," she said and exited into the chapel.

I raced through vesting and followed the young boy out onto the altar, thinking that I had to work on inspiring more respect in my fellow religious. Between Brother Tobias and Sister Louis, my clerical ego had been brought low.

The altar was miniscule, the altar wine *was* vinegar, and the altar boy actually fell asleep on his knees. But I persevered and brought my Lord Jesus down onto those humble boards with a fervor and joy that entirely surprised me. And when I distributed Communion and found Henriette Delille and two other colored women kneeling just behind the nuns, my morning was sanctified. Giving Communion to Miss Delille, I was seized by a strange sensibility — a feeling of privilege — something I have certainly never felt before. I went back to the altar with my spirit soaring, my, mind in a state of holy confusion. My thanksgiving after Mass was intense and lengthy and, in fact, continued all the way back to the Great Convent, where I fell on my knees just inside the door of my cell and gave thanks to my Lord Jesus for bringing me to New Orleans.

Brother Tobias served me a breakfast of soft-boiled eggs, salt pork, and toast with butter. There was wine on the table, but I poured the water, thinking to mortify myself after last night. One sip of the water and I reached for the wine. Mortification was one thing, but death by foul water was quite another. Tantamount to suicide.

"This water is polluted," I said to Brother Tobias.

"Yes, of course," he said, with a great Gallic shrug. "But not always. You must go by the nose. Sometimes it stinks, sometimes it does not."

"Thank you," I said.

"It is as nothing," he said, and went out.

I looked after him, thinking that this man is dourly dangerous. I must be careful what I take from his hands or I may very well die of the sulfurous bloat.

But the eggs were excellent.

EIGHT

Saturday

I was in my room reading some mail that had finally caught up with me when Brother Tobias put his head in at the door.

"You are wanted at the gatehouse," he said.

"Oh?"

"Three women." He eyed me closely. "They may be colored. They say they know you."

"Thank you, Brother. I'll see to it."

He withdrew, looking just slightly scandalized.

I went down to find Henriette Delille and the other two women to whom I had given Communion earlier that morning. Henriette introduced them as Juliette Gaudin and Josephine Charles. As I had mentally noted this morning, Miss Charles was quite beautiful, tall, stately of carriage. Miss Gaudin was short, busy-eyed, almost birdlike. They were dressed in the same heavy black bombazine dresses that Henriette wore, threadbare and bepatched.

"We have a problem, Father. And we are very sorry to disturb you."

Not at all. What is it?"

"A slave we have taken in from the streets is, I fear, very near death."

"I see."

"We have instructed her and given her conditional baptism but we would be pleased to see her given the last rites."

I hesitated. A slave? Was this canonically regular? If not, why not? "Of course," I said. "I'll fetch my oils."

And so it began — my ministry to the slaves of New Orleans streets, orchestrated by Henriette Delille and her friends: the Congregation of the Sisters of the Presentation of the Blessed Virgin Mary, as I soon came to know.

The stable they had expropriated for their infirmary was a wretched hovel in a wretched place (upper Bayou Street), but they had made it as clean as they could and made their patients as comfortable as their means would allow. There were two women, one in midlife, the other ancient. Both looked at me when I entered with what had to be sheer terror in their eyes. I spoke to them, but they pulled back from me and began to chatter at Henriette in what she said was Mandingo, an African tribal tongue. Miss Charles went to the ancient one, made comforting sounds, and indicated to me that this was the one who was dying.

I rebaptized both of them first, at Henriette's request and then turned my attention to the dying woman. She relaxed as I started the Latin of the ritual of confirmation in danger of death. The women, meanwhile, had laid out the cotton pellets on a white cloth, a crust of bread, and a small cruet of water, and had lighted a small candle. The women knew all the responses and attended the poor woman and me as I anointed the ears, the nostrils, the mouth, the hands and the feet and when I began to recite the *Domino sancte*, the three women recited it aloud with me. I was impressed and edified and very nearly yielded to the tears I felt growing in my eyes. When I offered her the cross, the dying woman seized it, kissing it devoutly over and over again. I left the stable with my head bowed to avoid the effusions of the women and to conceal the tears that I could feel now flowing down my face.

I walked home by way of Esplanade, the street of the slave sheds, on whose front steps and boardwalks the slaves were made to stand on exhibition from nine in the morning until four in the afternoon. Some of them were turned out rather elegantly: the women in calico dresses and brightly colored bandanas, and the men in broad cloth suits, with shirts and ties, polished shoes, and seven-inch beaver hats. These were, presumably, candidates for house slaves. The field hands were brought to the auction blocks in whatever grab-bag clothing happened to be handy and were often stripped of most of that in order to display their physical attributes. Every now and then I could hear the voice of a man — a boss or an owner or an auctioneer — issuing random commands, and you could see a stiffening in the ranks of the slaves.

I had stopped and was standing just across the street, wondering at man's inhumanity to man, when I was addressed by a gentleman who had paused beside me.

"Appalling, isn't it?"

"Yes," I said, and turned to look at him. A tall man, aquiline of feature, with wide-set gray eyes and an aspect you could only describe as fierce. He was dressed in a perfectly fitted black suit, gleaming boots, a tall beaver hat, and a luminous black silk cravat in which a dazzling diamond stickpin was centered. He was entirely too grand for an undertaker, rather too flashy for a clergyman, so I took him for a diplomat or perhaps a wealthy riverboat gambler.

"You, sir, are a man of the cloth, of the Romish persuasion to be sure, but a man of clear conscience nonetheless."

I smiled. His voice was a honeyed baritone, rich with theatrical embellishment. An actor, I thought. "I have a conscience," I said. "I try to keep it clear."

"Why then, sir, I have a request of you. I am a writer of sorts, and I have written a monograph about the current state of the city of New Orleans." He reached into an inside pocket and produced a slim pamphlet. "I would be greatly in your debt if you would do me the favor of reading it. Just read it. That's all I ask."

He handed me the pamphlet. I glanced at it. "Well, until I have seen the nature of it, I can't promise anything."

"You don't have to, sir. Just begin to read it. If you do that much, I can promise you it will seize and absorb your attention."

"Why, I certainly can promise that much."

"Thank you, sir. You will notice that it has been privately printed. That is because I could find no one in New Orleans to publish it. A brief examination will tell you why. It is the truth, sir, and no purveyor of the public prints in this city has even the least interest in the truth."

"I pray God that isn't the case."

"Believe it, sir. I swear it on my honor. I bid you good day, sir. I have a steamboat to catch, and other thousands to instruct."

He tipped his hat, bowed slightly at the waist, and went striding down the street, his coat tails flapping briskly behind him. I watched him until he turned a corner and disappeared.

To say that I was astonished wouldn't state it by half. As a priest, I have often been accosted on the public street, mostly by well-meaning persons who wish a blessing upon me or ask for a prayer, but sometimes by malefactors who cursed me or the pope or the Blessed Virgin. I've even been spat upon and struck from behind. But this was a first—to be addressed by a perfect stranger who was presuming to instruct me. And yet I have to confess that I could scarcely wait to get home to see what this little tract had to say.

It was about seventy pages in length, neatly enough printed, and divided into short chapters. The title was "New Orleans as It Is"

and "By a Resident" was the only clue as to the author. A few of
the chapter headings were sufficient to give me an idea as to what
was ahead:

"Concubinage"

"Kept Mistresses"

"Regular Prostitutes"

"Prostitution of Wives"

"A Man Selling His Own Children"

"Slave Girls as Bed Companions"

"Slavery"

"Apologies for Slavery"

"A Woman Whipped to Death"

"Chain Gangs of Women"

"Slave Market"

"Depravity of Slave Holders"

Reading these over, I began to feel like a seminarian who has
come across a copy of *Candide*. Would the cultural gain be worth
the risk of impure thoughts? Should I ask the dean? But, as at least
half a priest's life is dealing with depravity — and since this certainly
seemed like a short course in New Orleans's venery and vice — I
took the tract firmly by the preface and proceeded.

> In placing the following pages before the American public, no apology
> is necessary by the writer to excuse himself for the plainspoken manner
> in which he has given, in detail, the living character of "Life in New
> Orleans." The design has been from the beginning to draw a faithful
> picture of the heterogeneous mass of human beings who mingle
> together in this great charnel house, and to delineate as near as possible
> the demonstrations of human passion which, to a very great degree,
> lead on the devotees of pleasure, unchecked by moral force or example
> or precept such as is brought to bear upon the evils that do exist here.

A perfectly awful, prolix, almost maundering beginning. The man
said he would tell the truth, but he forgot to add that he was a
master of pleonasm.

Still, I pressed on, thumbing through to the end of the book, hoping that the long labor of the thing might have attenuated the flow of words. I opened to the chapter entitled "Slave Market."

Go to the slave market in New Orleans, in the Arcade, on days of auction sales for slaves, and you will see and learn what you cannot in any other place in the world.... For it is here before you in unmistakable character how completely unfeeling, inhuman, and brutalized a man can become, and yet be a *"gentleman"* and *"respectable."* And surely it would be *unkind* and *ungenerous* in the extreme to say that those *fine-looking, rich,* and *generous-hearted* men who stand there daily and *only* sell slaves, are not *"gentlemen"* or *"respectable."* And notwithstanding all the brutality which you see them exhibit, they claim to have in a large degree the common sympathies of our nature, as well as *moral sensibilities.* But an astonishment amounting to amazement comes over you when you view these men as they are truly exhibited here. You see before you a hundred men, women, and children of all ages, colors, and complexions, and many of them as white and even whiter than the auctioneer or the purchaser. You hear their rude jokes and loud laugh while describing the qualities and condition of some female, and you can see her shrink back and drop her head with the true feelings and sense of female delicacy: and yet this just rebuke upon them only calls out another rude joke as evidence of greater brutality.

And, a little later, he moved on to an eyewitness account:

To satisfy curiosity, in the fall of 18 —, I stepped into one of the rooms in which were about thirty slaves, principally girls, from the age of fifteen to twenty. I observed a fine-looking mulatto girl about seventeen years old and enquired into her qualities. The trader called her up and replied that "she was an excellent sewer and dress-maker, good body-servant and lady's waiting-maid and nurse, had a good disposition, was kind and careful with children, and was perfectly healthy and without a fault or blemish of any kind." After this description he said to her, "Put out your foot and pull up your clothes. See what a fine foot and ankle she has got." He then bid her turn around, and, putting his hands on her waist and hips, said, "See what beautiful form." And then, removing the slight covering from her neck, he remarked, "And what fine full breasts she has — she will raise at least eight children." And during all this *commonplace* exhibition, I closely watched the blood course through her veins and could discover a deep tinge of crimson flash over her cheek, and her eyes fell to the floor as evidence that she involuntarily shrank from the rudeness that was thus being forced upon her, while the trafficker in human flesh stood there as brutal and unfeeling as though every heart was as callous to moral sensibility as his own. I turned away with a shudder from the scene before me, ashamed of the curiosity that had prompted me to make this invasion upon female delicacy, and call out such an exhibition of human depravity as this trader presented, while her sense of propriety and delicacy had not even the privilege of covering her face, nor the apology of temptation.

Despite the ministerial tone and the fustian, I found myself deeply affected by these passages. This was what was going on every day, just outside the walls of our sanctuary. And there wasn't a thing we could do about it. This kind of behavior was so commonplace and accepted that it took an outsider to see anything wrong with it. And, as I was to discover over and over again, the voice of an outsider in New Orleans was so indignantly and vehemently dismissed that the outsider couldn't wait — as witness my friend Mr. Stickpin, as I dubbed him — to board the next outbound steamboat.

And I couldn't help but think of another friend, Henriette Delille, who, had she not been born a free woman of color, could easily have found herself on the block enduring the same kind of abject humiliation. This thought brought the whole business in upon me with such intensity that I fell to my knees, put my face in my hands, and burned with shame.

So much for the tough, sophisticated priest from Lyon who had come to set the New World straight.

❧ HENRIETTE ❧

NINE

The tide was high and Potter's Field was at half flood when they got there in late afternoon. Juliette and Josephine were up on the wagon box with Charles. Henriette was in back with the corpse.

"You know where to go, Charles," Henriette said.

"Yes'm," Charles said.

He turned the wagon left toward the only high ground at the farthest edge of the field. He pulled up at the boundary as the horse shied at a large snake moving toward the deep swamp.

"Go, you devil," Charles said. "You get no souls here today." The women took turns with one shovel while Charles worked expertly with the other. At three feet, the water came up two inches deep in the grave, and they stopped digging. The women went to the corpse, while Charles stood well to one side looking on with fear-rounded eyes. The corpse was wrapped in burlap, which began to rip as the women laid it in the grave.

Henriette took her place at the head of the grave and, the sweat running on her face, she spoke a prayer in a soft, steady voice.

"Here lies Abigail, a slave. She lived a hard life, and she died a hard death, with no kith or kin to attend her. So she comes to you, a Christian soul alone. Receive her, dear Father, and exalt her before your throne. And, dear God, because there will be such a long loneliness before the Resurrection, protect these remains, watch over this grave, keep it safe from tigers and thieves in the night and all those who would despoil it. Raise her up in glory, dear Father, into the company of the angels and archangels so that she may know that she was made in your image, made worthy of eternal peace in the holy light of your divine Eye."

The women murmured amen, and Charles came forward to join Juliette as she took up the shovel and began to fill in the grave. Henriette went to the wagon and returned with a small wooden cross and a cobblestone. She used the stone to hammer the cross into the ground at the head of the grave. "Abigail" had been carved into the transverse bar.

When the grave was filled and mounded, all stood at the foot, and Henriette said, "Go, Christian soul, to that place prepared for you from the beginning of the world. And flights of angels sing thee to thy rest."

As they rode out of the graveyard, the sun was huge in the west, and Henriette, seated again alone in the back of the wagon bed, began to weep softly. And she prayed: *Dear God, end this plague of slavery. Send Michael the Archangel with his broadsword, and end it in the holy name of Jesus.*

PART TWO

1838–1840

PART TWO

1838-1840

❧ HENRIETTE ❧

TEN

Father Rousselon greeted her with a broad smile and escorted her to a chair opposite his desk. He had been out in the parishes for the prior month, visiting the priests and the convents, and looked to Henriette as though his travels and the break from routine had entirely agreed with him.

"I hope you are well," he said, beaming at her as he seated himself behind the desk.

"I am, thank you, Father," Henriette said. "And you?"

"Never better," he said. "The diocese not only survives, it prospers."

"I am glad to hear it."

"And your work?"

"It . . . goes on. We have missed your presence, of course."

"I'll be available first thing in the morning. But first I have a very pleasant surprise. The Ursulines have graciously decided to donate to the diocese a piece of property that they own at the corner of St. Claude and Bayou Road. They request that we use it to build a new church to be called St. Augustine's."

"Why, that's wonderful. So close to Congo Square. It will bring Jesus to that neighborhood."

"It will indeed. And I'm very pleased to tell you that I have already discussed it with the bishop, and I will be pastor."

Henriette half rose from her chair, clapping her hands together. "Oh, dear God! My prayers are answered!" She immediately sat down again, lowering her eyes in embarrassment.

53

Father Rousselon smiled at her. "You have prayed for this, exactly?"

Henriette nodded. "Exactly," she murmured. "Just so."

"Well, then, I think you will be very pleased to hear that I suggested to the bishop that St. Augustine's would make an ideal center for the establishment of a lay community of Negro women. And the bishop agreed."

Henriette sat stunned. "This is true?"

"Yes. Of course, the bishop didn't say an *order* of Negro nuns. But I think we may dare hope?"

"Yes. Oh, yes," Henriette said.

"Now all we have to do is raise the money to build the church."

"We will," Henriette said fiercely. "We will raise it."

"God willing."

"He wills it, Father. I know he does."

"Then we'll have a beginning. For you and your companions."

"Thank you, Father. With all my heart, thank you."

"You give me too much credit. Thank the Ursulines."

"I will, Father."

"And then, perhaps, you will thank me for this."

He opened a desk drawer, took out a book bound in bright-red buckram. "A journal, Henriette. For you."

Henriette reached out as Father Rousselon extended the journal toward her and took it in both hands. She held it for a moment and then ran her fingers over the red leather and the gilt edging on the pages. "It's beautiful," she said. "How can I thank you?"

"By writing in it," he said. "By filling it with your spiritual thoughts. Your dreams, your battles, your...your dialogue with God."

Henriette smiled at him. "It might just prove to be a catalogue of bandages and burials."

"What could be better?"

"Thank you, Father. I will treasure it."

"No. Write in it."

"I will. Every day."

"No. no. It's not a diary. When God moves you. Only then."

And so I begin, Henriette wrote, *my dialogue with God.*

What bold presumption. And yet . . . I shall presume. And I will dedicate every word of it to the Father, the Son, the Holy Ghost, and, especially to Blessed Mary, Mother of God. For I hang in this world as on a thread over the fires of hell, and without grace I would surely fall. Sustain me, dear God, and empower me, for I have set myself a long, harsh road, and I will not arrive without your holy hand upon me. And upon my sisters, Juliette and Josephine. Give them the strength to persevere, for it is so hard, so very hard.

Of slaves dead and dying there is no end. And we only are able to concern ourselves with the female slaves. And yet we are overwhelmed. We have only two rude beds, but there are often two and three lying on the floor. We do our best with them all, nurse them and pray with them. But so far, not one has survived. This is, of course, due to the fact that they do not want to live. They have had quite enough of life. Forgive them, Father, for they have never known true life. Never known joy, or security, or hope of anything better. It is why I often weep over them and beg them to believe that there is such a thing as a happy life without constant worry about being whipped, or raped, or made to watch while their children are scourged or bludgeoned, or taken away from them in the night. Dear God! I cannot convince them of heaven — they cannot conceive of it, they cannot imagine that such goodness awaits them! Do not fail them, dear Lord, whatever their sins, for I have told them that you will be waiting for them with golden chariots when they come to heaven's gate. You must be there when they arrive, dear Lord, and your loving arms will suffice if golden chariots are not the way of things in heaven.

I have one other favor to ask of you tonight, dear God. We are very short of medical things. We have run out of sheets to tear up for bandages. And the women are in dreadful need of bandages so that the flies will not swarm over their open wounds. We have taken to begging old bandages from the hospitals and boiling them for our purposes, but the hot water causes the bandages to turn to a gauzy mush so that they can hardly be wrapped around anything. And laudanum, dear Lord, so that we can ease their pain and keep them from screaming in the night. My God, you have heard their cries, their begging to die, their beseeching us to put them to death! I know it is expensive, dear and merciful God, but send us laudanum if it be within the province of your divine will.

That is enough for now. I am not a holy person and have no business addressing you in this manner. Please forgive my arrogance. But I am set upon a course that will require me to speak to you boldly, beseechingly, and I ask you to hear not my abrasive tone but only the surging in my soul and heart for your mercy upon the little ones of this earth. I yearn for you, I die for you, I give you my heart burning with love. Goodnight, dear and almighty God. Henriette.

She closed the book, sat for a few seconds, and then opened it again.

And, dearest God, rain down blessings upon the Ursulines.

Henriette was walking east on Burgundy Street when, at its intersection with St. Philip Street, she heard the girl screaming. She crossed to the head of an alley behind a boarding house. About halfway down the alley, a tall, light-skinned black man was holding the girl against the wall with one hand while slapping her across the face with the other. The girl was bleeding from the nose profusely, and, as she caught a glimpse of Henriette, she screamed, "Please help me!"

Without the least hesitation, Henriette strode down the alley. "Get away from her, you brute!"

The man turned and growled at Henriette. "This here is private business, lady. Get on out of here."

"It is not!" the girl cried. "He's a pimp who's trying to make me work for him!"

"I told you it was private," the man said.

"If you strike her again, I will have you arrested and prosecuted."

"How you goin' to get the *po*-lice?"

"I will blow my whistle and they will come immediately." Henriette reached into the bodice pleats of her black dress and grasped the large silver crucifix she wore around her neck. Covering it with her hand, and asking God to forgive her the lie, she brought it to her lips.

The man stepped away from the girl. "Okay, lady, okay. Take her. She ain't no use to me anyways."

"I want you to walk away from her."

"Surely will, lady." Then he turned to the girl. "I catch you working alone, bitch, you a dead woman."

"Go!" Henriette said.

The man looked around at her, shook his head. "I'm goin'. But you blow that whistle, and *you* is a dead woman." He glowered at Henriette for a moment and then turned and walked away down the alley.

The girl sagged against the building. "Oh, my God," she said. "Thank you, thank you."

"Get yourself together," Henriette said. "He might come back. Come, come. We must walk briskly."

Henriette took her by the arm and propelled her down the alley and out onto St. Philip Street. She glanced back into the alley, but the man had gone out of sight. She turned to the girl and handed her a handkerchief. "Here. Wipe your nose."

The girl was a quadroon, a free woman of color, huge-eyed and pretty. Her name was Maria Pellerin, and she had run away from her home on the Cane River.

"Why did you run away?" Henriette asked. They were seated in the living room of the Delille house, having tea. Maria had cleaned herself up and looked quite at home with her teacup poised just above the saucer.

"To get away from my stepfather."

"He was cruel to you?"

"He tried to have his way with me."

"I beg your pardon?"

"He tried to rape me. Twice."

"Oh, dear Lord," Henriette said. "And your mother? Couldn't she—"

"My mother is dead."

"Oh, I'm so sorry."

"I think he killed her. I think he drowned her in the river."

"Dear God. You poor child."

"Not so poor. I took some of his money that he kept in a box under his bed."

"I see." Henriette felt the strain of taking all of this in at one sitting.

"He was in the bed when I took the money, but he didn't hear me because I think he had already died in the night. He was seventy-one, and there was this smell in the room."

"He died...of natural causes?"

"Pardon?"

"I mean, if he was dead, you did nothing to cause it?"

"Oh, no. It was the whiskey that killed him. He drank whiskey all day, half the night. If it hasn't killed him yet, it will."

Henriette sighed and looked away. What was she to do with all of this? With this girl? Why had God put such a perplex in her path? She turned back to the girl. "And this man who was beating you? Where did he come from?"

"He was at the dock when I got off the steamboat. I refused his offer to carry my bags. I have two carpetbags."

"Where are they?"

"At the rooming house."

"You took a room?"

"Yes. Then I got very hungry and thought I would go out and get something to eat. I looked up and down the street because I wondered if he had followed me. I didn't see him, so I went out. And as I went by the alley, he grabbed me and pulled me in."

"He'd followed you up from the dock?"

"Yes. But I can run, and I ran a little and got ahead of him."

"He pulled you into the alley and began to beat you?"

"Well, not right away. First he tried to kiss me. Then he told me he could introduce me to lots of nice gentlemen. And all he wanted was half of what they gave me. For his trouble. And when I said no, he began to hit me and say that he knew what I was, a street girl, and he wasn't going to let me run loose in his territory. That's when I knew he was a pimp. Or wants to be a pimp."

"How do you know, at your age, what a pimp is?"

"My half-brother, Blaise, is a pimp. In Plaquemines Parish. He also tried to put me in his employ."

"Good Lord. I scarcely know what to say."

"Well, it is not your concern. You have been very kind and very brave. You saved me from a terrible situation. And I am very grateful. But I think I have bothered you long enough." She put down her cup and saucer. "I will take my leave now and go back to my room."

Henriette felt a surge of relief. Perhaps this could end satisfactorily after all. "Well, I can't let you go alone. I'll walk back with you. I have business in that direction, as it happens."

"You do? Truly?"

"Yes."

"What do you do? I mean, your business?"

"Well," Henriette said, wondering how she could explain her 'business' to this girl. "I do what I can to . . . help the poor."

Maria stared at her. "I notice you dress in black. Not fashionably at all. Are you a nurse?"

"I will explain as best I can. As we walk."

"Very well," Maria said. She stood up. "I have the money in my red carpetbag. I want you to have some of it. For your poor."

"We will talk about that, too," Henriette said, getting to her feet, thinking: *God help me to get out of this gracefully.* "I think you will be needing every penny to get yourself established."

"Oh, I don't think so," Maria said. "I have over three thousand dollars."

"That is a lot of money. Don't you think your stepfather may be coming to look for you?"

"It was my mother's money, and she meant for me to have it. He simply stole it from me. That's the truth. And if he comes looking for me, I will go to the authorities. I have a copy of my mother's last will and testament."

Henriette, impressed with her matter-of-fact demeanor, smiled. "And if he comes after you, we will confront him, and I will threaten to blow my whistle."

Maria smiled. "You don't really have a whistle, do you?"

"No."

"You are so brave. To face that pimp down like that."

"It was my faith in God, not bravery. If you stand to it, evil will not prevail. God will not allow it."

"You are that sure?"

"I have staked my life upon it."

As they walked, Henriette explained about the slave women left destitute and dying on the New Orleans streets and how she and her two friends took them in, cared for them, buried them when they died. Maria listened to every word, her eyes rounding in admiration. When Henriette paused, she said, "You truly are a holy woman. I would like to help you. I would be honored."

"Honored? It is very difficult," Henriette said.

"I took care of my mother when she was sick. Sick to death. She wasted away to near a skeleton. Which is why he killed her. She just wasn't dying fast enough for him."

"You have been through some dreadful things."

"Yes, and I believe. I purely do. I pray to Mary and Jesus every night. And I'm strong. I can carry my own weight."

Henriette smiled. "Yes, I'm sure you can. And I do appreciate your offer to help." She glanced at Maria. She was a strapping girl, certainly not delicate, and apparently not afraid. Why not? "Well," Henriette said, "I tell you what we'll do. You get a good night's sleep, and we will talk again tomorrow."

"Oh, thank you."

"I will come for you about this same time and take you to the infirmary. Then you will get an idea."

"Is that where you're going now?"

"Yes, but I'm afraid we'll have a burial to do. I'd have no time to talk to you. Tomorrow will be much better."

"Yes, ma'am."

Henriette saw her into the rooming house, arranged with the buxom proprietress for some dinner to be brought in to Maria, and left, assuring Maria that she would not be forgotten or neglected.

"That pimp comes in here, he'll wish he hadn't," the proprietress said, producing a short club from under the counter.

"I'm much reassured," Henriette said.

"I'll knock his goddamned head in," the proprietress said.

"I have every confidence in you," Henriette said, and went out thinking that what God might damn had been accurately assessed in this case.

They did have a burial, short and simple because Father Rousselon was not available to preside. And afterward, Henriette told Juliette and Josephine about the Ursulines' property gift and the possibility of a new church.

"Our church," Henriette said. "Or, at least, the center of our activities."

"Did the Ursulines say that?"

"No. But Father Rousselon did. And he will be pastor."

"Did he say we would be an order?"

"No, Josephine. But it is a beginning. A necessary beginning for us."

"Yes," Juliette said. "And who is to pay for the building of this church?"

"We must raise the money."

"Oh sure. Of course," Juliette said. "We might as well try to raise St. Augustine."

"We must try, Juliette," Henriette said. "We must try desperately."

"Yes," Juliette said. "That's the word."

"Well," Josephine said. "I know some people who might contribute toward building a church. They might not contribute toward supporting three women who are plucking poor slaves out of gutters. But a church, why that's another matter."

"Of course it is," Henriette said. "And we can put the contributors' names up on the walls on those little brass plaques.

Cover the walls with them! And they will sit in the pews and hum pleasantly, just knowing that they are publicly acknowledged as church-builders."

"Yes," Juliette said. "I know some people like that. Not well, but I know them. Well enough to ask for money."

"Good!" Henriette said. "Then we are resolved."

"We are!" Josephine said.

"It is as it is," Juliette said.

❧ ETIENNE ❧

ELEVEN

Friday

Sitting alone this afternoon in the high-ceilinged hall of the Great Convent, the heat intense, the sweat pouring down underneath my soutane — even into my shoes — I thought about religious vocation. And what an overwhelming commitment it routinely requires. That it is contrary to human nature, there can be no question. One pledges to deny the natural instincts of one's body, one's mind, and even one's soul — if the soul has even the minimum of vagrant feelings and inclinations that might be called self-indulgent. One must sacrifice every tiniest natural disposition to the ideal — the mystical body of Christ. I am a member of that mystical body, and any least turning away betrays that membership, ever so slightly. And any major turning betrays it utterly. Cut off from all grace, cast into the outer darkness, the soul withers and, looking in from a great distance, watches the light inexorably fail until the slightest gleam is gone. Then the soul experiences the desolation of desolations: despair.

Any of us can reduce ourselves to despair. But the person called to the religious life, who has received the special graces thereunto appertaining, and who has yet turned away, spurned God's grace, defied God's best efforts to infuse that person's soul with saving grace...well, that person has chosen hellfire and richly deserves it.

And yet, even that person, in the middle of his or her last half-step into hell, can be saved. A nun who has taken a demon lover, a priest who has celebrated a black mass — even these, if they will only turn and say, "My Lord and my God," will be snatched back from the abyss, will — however long their purgatories — be assured of one day looking upon the holy face of God.

64

I marvel at these things. I marvel at the incredibly magnanimous mercy of God. He refuses to be implacably denied; he refuses to give over any soul, even unto the last split-second of human defiance. He is strong to save, and the gates of hell will not prevail against him.

Why do I write this meditation? What made it imperative? I will confess without qualm or qualification. It was the face of Henriette Delille when I gave her Communion this morning at Mass. After three-and-a-half weeks away from her — twenty-five days of disporting myself around the parishes as the next thing to the bishop himself, reveling in my power and the pomp that it provoked — I looked into her face and realized what a religious dandy I am. Her expression was beatific, divinely infused, and I saw in her eyes the forgiveness of God, the absolute serenity and mercy and patience of our Lord and Savior Jesus Christ.

I do not exaggerate. I do not imagine. I do not equivocate. She is an imperially noble and holy soul — one who would seize the hand of her assassin, smile upon him, and tell him in her last breath to get to confession as soon as possible to receive God's blessing lest he lose his immortal soul.

Thank God that my vision, distorted as it must be by my own asinine pretensions, does not blind me to this young woman's holiness. She will not only accomplish the salvation of the most wretched derelict's soul in the foulest ditch in New Orleans, she may even, God help me, accomplish the salvation of mine.

God make me worthy of her trust. God save me from that last half-step and from anything that might dismay her.

Amen.

❧ HENRIETTE ❧

TWELVE

"Why there's almost four thousand dollars here," the man in the bank said, looking out at Henriette and Maria. "You miscounted by eight hundred and seventy-seven dollars."

"Well," Maria said. "I never actually counted it before."

The man nodded. "All right. How do you want this account to read?"

"Maria Pellerin and Henriette Delille."

"Wait, wait," Henriette said. "You mustn't do that."

"Yes, I must, Henriette. I want us to share it equally. It is only fitting. Please let me do it. You've seen my mother's will. You know it's my money."

"I don't question that. You'll be needing your money to support yourself."

"I want to join you in your work."

"Ladies," said the bank teller. "If you please?"

"Very well," Henriette said. "Do as she says." Then, to Maria, "but there is nothing final about this. Once you see what my work is, you are likely to have second thoughts."

"I don't think so," Maria said. "All of my life I have wanted to do a holy thing. Now God is offering it to me."

Henriette blinked. "All your life? How old are you, Maria?"

"Nineteen."

"Well, you might have a vocation. We'll put it to the test."

"Which one is Pellerin?" the man said.

"I am," Maria said.

"Here's your book. And here's yours," he said, handing each a small bank book.

"Thank you," Maria said.

"I thank you, Maria," Henriette said. *And St. Augustine thanks you,* she thought.

When they got to the shelter, Juliette was bathing a new arrival.

"This one has been shot. He is near dead."

"*He?*" Henriette said. "You have taken in a man?"

"They brought him to us," Juliette said. She rolled the man over. There was a large exit wound in his lower abdomen. But there was no question about his being a man.

"Cover him up," Henriette said.

"We really can't move him," Josephine said. "He will start bleeding again."

"Well, either he goes or we do," Henriette said.

As Juliette put a towel over the man's thighs, Henriette looked around at a noise she heard behind her.

"Oh," Josephine said.

Henriette turned. Maria had fainted and collapsed to the floor just behind her. Henriette bent to her and, as Josephine came over to help, she said, "This is Maria. She says she wants to become one of us."

"She says what?" Juliette said. "Well, she'd better get hold of her vapors first. I mean, the last thing we need is any more folks lying around in a heap on the floor."

"Charity, Juliette, charity," Josephine said.

"She just gave almost two thousand dollars to the church fund," Henriette said.

"She *did?*" Juliette said. "Why then prop that girl up and give her some salts. "She just might prove out after all."

Later, when the man had been moved to Mercy Hospital and Henriette was satisfied that no visible scandal had occurred, the three of them sat in the shelter (there was only one slave woman under care) and discussed Maria Pellerin.

"Are we sure she is still interested?" Josephine said. "After seeing the wounded man?"

"Oh, yes," Henriette said. "She couldn't stop apologizing for her... sensibility."

"Oh, I think she'll do," Juliette said. "She didn't ask for her money back."

"No, of course not." Henriette said.

"So," Juliette said. "The only question is, has she got the stomach for it?"

"Well, I didn't, at first," Josephine said.

"You never fainted dead away," Juliette said.

"I came very close, that whole first month."

"So," Henriette said, "we are agreed to give her a chance?"

"I like her spirit," Josephine said.

"I like her dowry," Juliette said.

Later, alone in her room, Henriette wrote:

I don't know what it is that makes me hesitate so about Maria Pellerin. Is it her stepfather, and the possibility of his coming after her? No, no. I will stand ready to protect her, to go to the law and have him restrained. I don't think it's that. No, I think it lies deeper. Something about taking the responsibility for her—for her and any young woman who might apply to us. If this is the truth, I must surely examine it carefully. Do I want to establish an order of black sisters? I certainly do. But am I ready to assume leadership? To take them under my charge, and instruct them, and mold them, and make them proper daughters of God, brides of Christ?

I think I am suffering a failure of confidence. A lack of enabling grace. I have been neglecting my prayer, my meditation. Surely I know that God will sustain me, bolster me up if my cause is just in his holy eyes. And it must be just. God help, me! Am I simply being willful? Is it possible that God does not want an order of black nuns just now? Or ever? Are we worthy of such an ambition?

Dear God, hurry to my assistance! I falter, I falter! Holy God and my Lord Jesus Christ, make me steadfast, give me the grace of perseverance. If that is your divine will.

PART THREE

1841–1842

❧ ETIENNE ❧

THIRTEEN

Sunday

A special event this morning. I was walking past the front of the cathedral on my way home when I saw a handsome young black man, dressed in rags, standing next to a fountain at the top of Jackson Square. While I watched, he produced a shiny brass trumpet from behind his right leg, brought it smartly to his lips, and, pointing it upward toward the cathedral spires, played "Amazing Grace." Played it with such a fullness and purity of tone, with such startling intensity and emotion and firmness of line, that I was transfixed: stood stock still staring until he had lowered the trumpet, turned, and walked slowly south toward the levee.

I wanted to run after him, as two little street urchins were doing, and ask him his name, his address, and where he had learned to play like that. But, of course, I did not. And this was partly because I felt I had just been witness to a very personal and private ceremonial, and that to intrude upon his moment in any way would be an inexcusable rudeness.

But I haven't stopped thinking about him. I wonder if he is a slave — he almost certainly is — and I wonder if he knows that the author of the hymn, John Newton, had once commanded a slave ship. Newton had been converted by an "amazing grace" and became an Anglican priest and preached against slavery from his pulpit at St. Mary Woolnoth in London for twenty-five years before his death in 1807 — the very year in which slavery was abolished in England. I thought that the young black man ought to know these things, and I resolved to keep an eye out for him whenever I was in the vicinity of the cathedral.

My happiest duty in the diocese concerns my sponsorship of the works and ambitions of Henriette Delille. She is determined to found an order of black nuns, and I am determined to help her. Antoine is sympathetic but cautious. The three "Sisters of the Presentation" (as their informal congregation is called) may be quite holy enough, but what about future recruits? What if Miss Delille decides that she wants to enroll slaves? Or ex-slaves? She will, but I didn't tell Antoine that. Education, religious and otherwise, among the free women of color is amazingly good. Among the slaves and ex-slaves, however, it is virtually nonexistent. Henriette should be the first to know this, but she says if the mind and soul are pure, God will see to the rest, and that she is not thinking of an order of physicians and surgeons. Although she could use a few of both.

As for Henriette herself, she continues to astonish. She is absolutely resolute in her purpose and unrelenting in her devotion to the slaves. I have awakened on foul winter mornings with the Great Convent rocking and the wet wind cold enough to freeze up your nose, and I have lain there in my bed telling myself that there was no way under heaven that I could arise from the warmth of my blankets and go about my priestly duties. And then I would think of Henriette, and I would *know* that she was out there on the miserably cold streets tending to this or that wounded soul, heaving them up out of their filth and misery and taking them to one or the other of her wind-blasted havens, tending to them as best she could, and fully expecting that, if death were nigh, good Father Rousselon would be there in God's name and without fail to administer the last rites. And she almost never failed me.

What astounds me most, of course, is her own stamina and good health. She is a frail person, almost delicate of physique, but she is strong. She has held her little congregation together by sheer force of will. And it is no exaggeration to say that Antoine and I have come to rely upon the "Sisters" of the Presentation. They do things for the poor and destitute and dying that no one else does (there are two or three other groups of "pious ladies" doing pious works, but none of them so resolute as Henriette's band of angels), and have become so important to us that, last year, Antoine sent a request to Rome that the Sisters of the Presentation be affiliated with the Sodality of the Blessed Virgin Mary in Rome. Rome approved, which allowed the women in New Orleans to participate in the indulgences or special blessings granted to the sodality. Henriette was delighted with this recognition and showed me where she had listed the indulgences in her prayer book. And I have no doubt that, emboldened by this recognition, she will begin to press ever more firmly for recognition as a formal religious order. The first step will be for the women to have a house of their own in which to live in community. I am already working on this.

I have been Henriette's confessor for the past several years. I don't think it violates the seal for me to say (in this private journal) that I am stunned by her holiness. And we have had conversations outside of the confessional that confirm this estimation. She once brought up, for example, that she thought that one of her most serious faults was inattentiveness to the voice of God. I joined this conversation very carefully, not sure whether she was talking about actually hearing the voice of God (which really wouldn't have surprised me), or hearing his voice, as most of us do, indirectly through what we experience and observe in the course of any given day. I'm relieved to say she meant the latter; I couldn't have dealt very expertly with the former. But what concerned her was that she could sometimes pass two or three hours of her waking day without consciously directing herself to attend to what God might want of her. And this without the least hint of scrupulosity. I wrestled with it as best I could, telling her that it was certainly not sinful, perfectly natural, and so on. But I remember how she looked at me, as from across a great gulf. Where she is, where she lives, answers such as mine are irrelevant. She is not concerned about the possibility of her sinning; she is concerned about mystical union with God, total absorption in the mystical body of Christ. God help me: I am dealing with a saint.

FOURTEEN

Monday

God has chosen to send me a new trial. He is Father Jacques Pinchot, a graduate of my own seminary in Lyon. He has now been with us a little less than three weeks, and it already seems like three years.

He is a high-strung, nervous young man of extraordinary academic achievement. His cultural interests are broad and intense, ranging from Etruscan pottery to Mayan wines, from Creole cooking to Native American burial practices. He is also an expert in French oenology and is apparently fascinated with voodoo and its practitioners. Just how he has found time to fit in any interest in his priesthood is problematical, but I don't think it troubles him much.

When he first arrived, I sized him up as a rather introverted young man, a scholar perhaps, and mistaking his intensity for holiness, I assigned him to the chaplaincy of the Ursuline Convent. He seemed pleased. This would give him ready access to New Orleans bookstores (all two of them) and, he hoped, time to visit all of the cultural and historic venues. He didn't mention the Ursulines and didn't seem to hear me when I mentioned Henriette Delille and her companions, to whom he is also chaplain.

He took the first week of his ministry off. He was seen here and there in the French Quarter during the day, and at all of the best restaurants during the evenings. Meanwhile his effects had begun to arrive from France. I have never in my life seen such a wretched excess of baggage and boxes and trunks assigned to one priest in my life. I counted three crates of cheese, perhaps fifteen crates of bottled wines, three crates of port wine from Oporto, and two great boxes of canned foodstuffs from a purveyor in Paris. There were three boxes from Spain, seven smaller boxes from Italy, and a fat little box of what I took to be candies from a confectioner in Belgium. There was, finally, a handsome chest of hammered metal with heavy handles and a large padlock from Havana, Cuba, which

I at first took to be rum but which later proved to be the very best of hand-rolled cigars.

I dutifully forwarded all of these to the convent and received back from the nuns little notes of inquiry about when Father Pinchot might start saying morning Mass and assuming his other duties. I ignored the first few of these, thinking that Pinchot would come round directly and all would be well.

But then on the eighth day I received a note from Henriette Delille saying that Father Pinchot had not made himself available for Mass, confession, baptisms, marriages, funerals, or anything else priestly within the last fortnight. And she wanted to know if he was a working priest, or if he was some kind of unfortunate whose faculties had been suspended. I set out immediately for the Ursuline School.

When Pinchot opened the door to his quarters — a spartan apartment of three small rooms in the west wall of the convent enclosure — I fell back in astonishment. He was wearing a brocade dressing gown in a color I can only describe as chartreuse, had a lighted cigar in one hand, a flute of champagne in the other, and an expression on his face of a falling angel caught in mid-descent. "Good morning, Father," I said.

"Oh, what a surprise. Yes. Good morning, Father. What a pleasure to see you. Of course." He stood there for a moment, blinking. Then said, "What can I do for you, Father? I mean, come in, come in. By all means."

I went in and stood in the middle of what used to be the humble sitting room of the priest-in-residence. I looked around, amazed. He had transformed the place into a warehouse of wines, foodstuffs, cigars, and books. Books knee-deep in all directions.

"I see you found our bookstores."

"Oh, yes. Actually, not very well stocked."

"Not anymore. I hope you left them enough to stay in business."

"Why, certainly, Father," he said, managing a small smile. "Can I offer you some champagne? Not properly chilled, but a fairly acceptable vintage."

"I think I'll refrain, Father. I have a heavy schedule today."

"Then may I offer you a chair?"

There was only one chair in the room: a very high-backed and very well-cushioned comb-and-splat Windsor chair painted in black and gold. I hesitated to approach it. "I don't think so, Father. I must be on my way. But I wondered, first, if all of your shipments have arrived."

"Why no, not entirely, Father. There is a cask of wine yet to show up."

"Oh? A cask."

"A small cask, Father."

"I see. Altar wine?"

"Oh, much more than altar wine. It is one of the world's finest. A Romanée-Conti."

"Well, then. I'll certainly keep an eye out for it."

"Thank you, Father. Is there anything else?"

"Yes, there is. I have a note from Henriette Delille saying that, while you have said the occasional Mass in the last ten days, you have declined to attend the sick, give extreme unction, or officiate at funerals. Is this true?"

"Why, no, Father, no. I was available at all times."

"Even for Miss Delille?"

"Well, Father, I was about to say, I was available for the regular parishioners. But Miss Delille is involved with slaves. Surely, I'm not expected to minister to slaves."

"Surely, you are, Father. Don't you believe that slaves have souls?"

"But, Father, they can scarcely be called Christians, let alone Catholics."

"They can be called children of God!" I could hear the anger in my voice, and I let it rise. "You will consider these to be fully entitled members of your parish, and you *will* tend to them as solicitously as circumstances allow. Do I make myself clear?"

"Yes, Father," he said, looking both surprised and not a little offended. "Does that include burials at the Potter's Field?"

"It especially includes burials at Potter's Field. And Miss Delille is to be treated with the greatest respect and deference. As you will come to know, she is a profoundly holy person and has the complete confidence of the bishop and myself. I expect you to honor that confidence." I paused. He looked like he'd been hit in the face with a shovel. "Have you any other questions?"

"No, Father, no. I didn't realize—"

"But now you do," I said.

"Yes, Father."

"Good." I turned to go and then glanced back. "Drinking champagne in the morning is not conducive to impeccable priestly conduct. I suggest you attenuate it severely."

He had just taken a long sip, and—caught between swallowing it or spitting it out—stood there, eyes popped like a blowfish. I left him just so.

❧ HENRIETTE ❧

FIFTEEN

Father Pinchot is a most indifferent priest. I can't speak of him as a man because I scarcely know him. His priestly manner is abrupt, foreshortened, almost angry, as if he were being dreadfully imposed upon by the least request and thoroughly resented the intrusion. I don't wish to judge him, but I sincerely do not know what to make of him. Hearing confessions, he starts saying, "Yes, yes," before I have gotten a word out, and fidgets and yawns throughout my recital, does not assign a specific penance (he simply says, "Do penance!"), and slams the slide shut with a report that is startling to say the least.

I hesitate to speak of this to Father Rousselon, <u>again</u>, but I fear I must. Not so much because of my personal reservations, but because of the way he performs his priestly functions. When he comes in to give the last rites to one of the slaves, he has at least two handkerchiefs soaked with lavender or lilac that overpowers every other smell in the room. Which is probably a blessing. But then he races through the rite, never touching the dying persons anywhere as is required, and finishes the ceremony with such speed that we are not sure how to make the responses or how to know he is finished until he puts his face in one of his handkerchiefs and walks out. He does come to the Potter's Field most of the time, but declines to approach the grave. Rather, he stands up on the road and, when we have placed the body in the ground, describes a sign of the cross in the air, says, "Requiescat in pace," and walks off.

*The brevity of his Masses is something of a scandal among us.
He is done in a little over fifteen minutes, moving so swiftly
on the altar that, at times, the chasuble seems to stand out
straight behind him as he moves from one side of the altar to
the other.*

*Reading over what I have written, I am somewhat ashamed
of myself. We are very fortunate to have him, and he has
obviously made great sacrifices in coming here. He is clearly
a young man of considerable wealth. There is even talk of his
being heir to a title in France. However true that may be, I
must stand by my criticisms. I would even go so far as to say
that it might be better to have no priest at all than to have
one who apparently has no interest in personal holiness and
no least concern for how a priest of Jesus Christ ought properly
to conduct himself.*

*If I had the courage, or the audacity, or whatever it might
require, I would speak to him myself instead of going to poor
Father Rousselon. But who am I — a nobody in the order
of things — to attempt to chastise a priest of God? A man
who has the power to bring Jesus down on the altar and to
cause him to be present in the Sacred Host? A man who has
the power in Christ to forgive sins? No, I cannot presume. I
will keep my place, and my thoughts to myself insofar as it is
possible. But Father Rousselon has no other way of knowing
what is going on if I do not tell him. So I must, at least once
more, be the tattletale. After that I will say no more. I will
simply redouble my prayers for Father Pinchot and hope that
the good Lord will move upon him and inspire him to take a
holy pride in his priesthood.*

SIXTEEN

Maria Pellerin smiled at Henriette. "Do you like my new dress?"

Henriette blinked at her and at the dress. It was long and black and suitably worn, but it was covered with sewn patches — some black, but mostly yellow, blue, brown, red, and a few that looked like they had been cut out of a piece of green velvet. "Well, it's certainly colorful," Henriette said.

"The landlady did it," Maria said. "I told her about having to find some suitable clothing, and she volunteered one of her own old dresses. We're about the same size, so she didn't have much altering to do. And she said she'd seen how you dress, and that she knew exactly what to do about the patches. But I guess she didn't notice that all of your patches are black or brown."

"It's all right, Maria. Even Joseph had a many-colored coat."

"But it *is* a bit...gaudy?"

"It will do nicely. We just might replace a few of the brighter ones." She paused, looking closely at the girl. "But, Maria, isn't this a little premature? I mean, are you already so sure you want to join us?"

"Oh, yes," Maria said with intensity. "Oh, yes, dear Henriette. I am absolutely certain. Those poor dear things." She looked past Henriette into the sick room of the little infirmary. "They need care. They need everything." She stopped, bringing one hand up to her mouth. "Oh! I almost forgot! I went to the apothecary and bought some things. Here!" She turned, went out the door, and then came immediately back in with a wooden box piled high with medical supplies. She set it down on a chair and began to pick through the contents. "Here is some laudanum, which I had to charm out of him. And here are bandages and salves and cotton balls and, best of all, this kit of medical instruments which I saw in a store window on Bourbon Street. They're not new but very clean, and they belonged to a doctor who died." She opened the kit and Henriette stared. A shiny, velvet-lined chest full of scalpels, forceps, scissors, probes, tissue clamps, and one vicious looking surgical saw.

"But, Maria—"

"Oh, and here's Epsom salts and smelling salts and some vegetal lilac, for the air."

"Yes, yes, but the cost, dear child. You can't go spending your money like this. You need it to live on."

"Oh, I have hundreds left. And I will live as you live. If you will have me."

"Well, of course, we will have you. But you must guard against an early enthusiasm." Henriette paused. "In a few weeks, or months, you may change your mind."

"If I do," Maria said, suddenly somber, "then God help me. For this is the most worthy possible thing I could ever do. I would be a fool to lose it. So I will not."

Henriette looked at Maria for a long moment, at her lovely, innocent face, her big-eyed eagerness to give and to give, and she smiled. "Dear Maria," she said. "God will help you. I think he loves you very much."

"You do? Oh, Henriette, I would die for God. Is that a proper thing to say?"

Henriette nodded. "That is a proper thing to say, Maria. And you have certainly come to the right place."

SEVENTEEN

"I'm afraid," Etienne said, "that he is a very sad example of a particular sort of young man who expected to be exalted and transformed by his ordination. He thought that once he was a priest all of his problems would be solved, all of his self-doubt obliterated. I have seen it before, many times. A young man trying to commit himself to the highest of ideals and then discovering that what he thought was commitment was a mere and vast vanity. Father Pinchot came here to conquer the world for Christ. I feel sure he had this dream. He would be the youngest bishop of the great territory, the crusader carrying Christ's word and cross to the American heathen. Instead, when he got here, he found our sophisticated squalor, our boredom with spirituality, our fascination with the thighs of depravity." He stopped short. "Pardon me, pardon me. I . . . I didn't mean to offend."

Henriette nodded solemnly. "Not at all, Father. You were quite eloquent. And accurate, I fear. The question remains, what are we to do about Father Pinchot? We need him here, and yet he will not take up his responsibilities."

"He will not take up his cross," Etienne said. "Until now, he thought of it as some sort of *noblesse oblige*. He has quickly discovered to his dismay that it is quite the other way around." Etienne smiled and nodded. "He has discovered that the true nobility in New Orleans resides with the humble, with the truly holy, such as you and your companions."

"Oh, Father," Henriette said, "you must not—"

"Yes, I must," Etienne interrupted. "If only to make my point." He looked at his hands splayed upon his desktop and pushed his lips tightly together. "Forgive me, Henriette, if I seem so certain. But I presided over a seminary for ten years in Lyon and saw dozens of such young men come and go. Dozens of proud, well-connected young men — even scions of minor nobility — come at the cross, struggle with its stark requirements, and fall back into secular life wondering whatever happened to the holy, shining cause of their forefathers. What happened to the Knights Templar, and the steed and the sword, and the deliverance of the holy city?"

He paused. "I may be exaggerating in the case of Father Pinchot. He hardly seems the militant, soldierly type. But his sensibility is the same. He wanted a crusade and he found a crucible. And it doesn't suit him at all, these small sacrifices day after day, year after year. He wants the grand gesture, however it may be constituted. The only way we could please him, perhaps, is to burn him at the stake." Father Rousselon smiled. "I've gone too far. But his romanticism carried me there. And if you are asking me what can be done about it, I simply do not know."

Henriette sat silent. Seldom had Father Rousselon been so eloquently impractical. The young priest must be sternly told to attend to his duties. That was it, plain and simple. She spoke. "Excuse me, Father, but I think it is all much less a matter of his dreams and disappointments than it is of his present failure to accept his lot, to gather himself, and to do what his priestly vows require him to do."

"Of course."

"And he must be most explicitly told to get himself in order, or to expect severe sanctions and his possible return to France without ceremony." Henriette paused, looking slightly dismayed. "We need him, Father, desperately. But we can certainly do without him."

Father Rousselon regarded her fondly for a moment and sighed heavily. "Thank you, Henriette, for putting it all in a clear light. You are right, of course, and I will address Father Pinchot apostolically as soon as I can fetch him over here."

"Thank you, Father."

"No. Thank you. You are my voice of brevity and clarity, and I owe you more than I can briefly state."

"Then, let it be, Father," Henriette said, smiling a tiny smile. "I must get back to my slaves."

❖ ETIENNE ❖

EIGHTEEN

Wednesday

I have learned that the wine in Father Pinchot's missing cask — the Romanée-Conti — is from a village in the Côte de Nuits district of Burgundy. That it is called Romanée-Conti after a Roman ruin and the prince de Conti, who acquired the vineyard in 1760. That it is made from pinot noir grapes and is one of the most expensive wines in the world. That the twelve gallons, more or less, in the small keg are easily worth a thousand dollars American, maybe twice that. And that the wine is so rare that, were it not for his distant relationship to the prince de Conti himself, Father Pinchot would never have come into its ownership.

I have, therefore, determined that Father Pinchot shall not have the wine, if and when we receive it or find it, and that it shall properly be donated to the bishop's table. And I truly believe that in enforcing this decision I shall force Father Pinchot to face up to his true values, to accept the penance the confiscation of the wine implies, and to either straighten out his life or get on the next boat.

It was, of course, fitting that I discuss this with Antoine before I announced it to Pinchot. So I brought it up over dinner tonight. We were, as it happened, drinking a *vin ordinaire* that must have gone over the hill shortly after the Battle of New Orleans. A discussion of a fine wine seemed salutary. When I had done with my preliminary explanation, Antoine nodded and said that he had once had a wine at the episcopal residence in Rouen that was from the same vineyard and was called La Tache.

"I had but one glass," he said. "And a half one at that. It was represented as one of the finest wines in France, and one of the

86

dearest. And, having tasted it, I daresay it was. Then I was told that it was one of the lesser wines of this particular vineyard, and that the premier wine was called Romanée-Conti."

"Do you think this missing cask might be worth a thousand American dollars?"

"At least. Have you searched the premises?"

"From the ground floor up."

"Well, let us search again."

"And if we find it?"

Antoine shrugged and smiled. "I certainly think we ought to taste it. To make sure it hasn't been damaged in travel."

"I agree. And, if it proves to be in good condition, I think it ought to be requisitioned for the bishop's table. If only to teach this young priest some humility."

"Which, from what I've been told, he sorely needs."

"I would say he needs it desperately. Either that or a ship back to Lyon."

"Oh, Lord, don't say that. We need *him* desperately."

"So? Do you want *him* to have the cask?"

"Well, why not do this? If the cask turns up, you and I will open it and sample it. Then we will invite him to dinner, serve the wine, and get him in a receptive mood for a no-nonsense lecture from me."

"He may still get angry."

"He will regret it if he does. I have every right to determine just what it is my pastors are drinking."

I smiled. "You are a man of great practical wisdom."

"Just as it should be, with an impoverished bishop." Antoine returned my smile, and we toasted our resolve with sour Beaujolais.

Just as a precaution, Brother Tobias and I searched the Great Convent carefully, virtually ransacking the ground floor. We did find a small cask, but it was clearly marked as white wine vinegar. We also found a pile of rusted handcuffs and ankle chains.

"My God," I said. "Did the nuns keep slaves?"

"Long enough to get their chains off," Brother Tobias said.

"They were tough people, those nuns."

"They still are," Brother Tobias said, spitting neatly into the center of a hand shackle.

My torch was almost exhausted. "I think we'd better call this off," I said. "If the cask ever got here, it will turn up and will be better for the aging."

"It never got here," Brother Tobias said. "And if the new priest says anymore about it, I — with your permission — will give him a swift kick in the crupper."

I grinned. "You'd kick a priest?"

"I'd kick this one, and God would forgive me," Brother Tobias said.

"I believe he would," I said. "And I would give you absolution."

NINETEEN

Saturday

Josephine Charles, saying she could not find Father Pinchot, came to fetch me about four o'clock this afternoon, saying that there was a slave woman very close to death at the "sisters'" infirmary. I packed my oils and followed her. She led me to a new place — a lean-to shed behind a stable — typical of the refuges the three women had lately been using. It was built of rough planks, with two straw-matted beds on either side of the front room.

As we entered, I saw an unfamiliar young woman standing over by the back wall, wearing a dress that looked like a carnival in black and primary colors. Henriette, bending over the bed of one of the patients, immediately came away to greet me. She murmured a hello, distractedly, then motioned me toward the bed of the other patient. The old woman was emaciated, little more than a skeleton, and as far as I could see, was already dead. I administered the last rites and tried to hear the woman's confession. But, although her eyes fluttered as I anointed them, she gave no further sign of life.

The stench in the room was almost intolerable, and, as I turned toward the other bed, I saw why. The other patient's right leg was swollen to three or four times its normal size, covered with ulcers and oozing pus. Henriette had returned to ministering to her, and, while I watched, she — with a pair of delicate forceps — was coaxing the head of a pearly-white worm out of the side of the leg, stretching it until it reached the length of six or eight inches. The worm appeared to be stuck, but finally came free with a sucking sound. Henriette threw it to the floor and stepped upon it firmly.

I stood aghast, utterly aghast, especially as I saw Juliette and Josephine moving the sidetable to the bed of the second woman. They began preparing her for anointing as well. My priesthood, then and there, underwent its severest test. I almost bolted from the room.

"Good Lord," I said to Henriette. "You could get a terrible infection."

"Well, the poor woman. She says they drive her crazy in the night."

"But is she dying?"

"We are afraid so," said Juliette. "The gangrene is almost to her groin."

I stood there looking at them, marveling at their intrepidity, their calm acceptance of these incredibly disgusting circumstances. And I remember saying to myself: Rousselon, what manner of man are you? What manner of priest? Gird up your sorry loins and do your sacramental duty.

And I did, but I am not sure how. And when it was all done, I staggered from the place into the half-light of the late afternoon and simply stood there, looking up at the impassive sky, wondering if I could possibly be made of the same stuff as those three dear women. Perhaps so, but their stuff was of a distinctly sterner quality than mine.

After dinner, I told Antoine of my afternoon visit to the infirmary. As I finished, he was looking at me with something like panic in his eyes.

"Oh, yes," he said. "Elephantiasis. And acute filariasis. Which brings on the worms. Dreadful business."

"Why, Antoine. How do you know the medical terminology?"

"I did my time among the slaves," he said. "And so did my dear friend, Dr. Maritain. Until he died of it."

"I had no idea," I said.

Antoine didn't want to talk about it. He excused himself soon after, and the matter was never raised again between us.

❧ HENRIETTE ❧

TWENTY

Henriette stood in the hallway of her sister's house weeping quietly. The doctor was in with Cecile, and she could hear his shrill voice saying, "Madam, you must put those rosary beads aside. You must allow me to examine your chest!" She could hear Cecile reply, but in a voice so small Henriette couldn't make out the words. But she knew what Cecile was saying: that she was going to die and that there wasn't anything the doctor could do about it. Cecile had said much the same thing to Father Rousselon, who had come to administer the last rites less than an hour before. Cecile had told the priest that she was resigned. But Henriette had read the frightened look in her sister's eyes, dull with dread. At thirty-four years of age, Cecile Delille was dying young and dying hard, and Henriette blamed herself, at least in part, for the latter.

The simple fact was that Henriette had never been able to give approval of Cecile's "arrangement" with Samuel Hart. It was, of course, accepted practice in Creole society. The quadroon girl was raised with the implicit expectation that she would enter into a liaison with a white man, bear his children, and never object if he took a white wife and had another set of children. This was the norm, not seriously challenged by the church, though some priests spoke up now and then to little effect. But Henriette was never persuaded, and, although she had not directly said so to Cecile, she thought it an evil business, mortally sinful, with the production of children its only saving grace. Samuel Hart had once asked her early on if she wouldn't care to join Cecile and him for an evening out with a dear friend of Hart's whom she might find agreeable. Henriette had answered coldly; she hadn't time for evenings out, and even less time for Hart and his friends. When Hart died suddenly in the epidemic of 1832, Henriette had gone to his funeral with Cecile and the children but had not mourned and did not pretend to.

The door to Cecile's room opened and the doctor stepped into the hallway with Betsy behind him. He was a small man with a tiny moustache, and the shine of his black wig almost exactly matched that of his black patent leather medical bag. As Betsy closed the door, he put a handkerchief to his nose and addressed Henriette.

"She is very low. I've done everything I can. Let me know if she lasts the night." And he went down the stairs humming to himself.

Betsy walked quickly to the banister and called down after him. "You just let yourself out, Mister Doctor! And if it's up to me, you ain't comin' back in again!"

"Betsy!" Henriette said. "He's doing the best he can."

"Yes, he is, and that's nothin'! We might better have called in the voodoo lady!"

"Betsy, that's enough. Now you go down and make some strong tea. I'll be in with Miss Cecile."

Betsy went down the stairs muttering to herself. Henriette crossed to the bedroom door, knocked gently, and went in.

Cecile blinked her eyes open as Henriette approached the bed. Cecile's eyes were full of awful apprehension. "Oh, Henriette, you must pray for me," she said. "I'm going to die this afternoon."

Henriette sat down in a chair by the bed and took her sister's hand. "Only God knows when we are going to die," she said.

"No, Henriette. I know it. I can see my death already. He is over there, waiting by the window. He's indulging me because of you and your prayers, but he is growing very impatient."

"You are imagining this, my dear Cecile."

"No, it is exactly as I say." She looked toward the window. "Now he nods his head firmly."

"Cecile, pray with me."

"It won't do any good, Henriette. God is not pleased with me. When I go to him, he is going to judge me very harshly."

"Cecile, stop this." Henriette was startled by the anger in her voice. "I'm sorry," she said. "Dear Cecile, you must believe in the mercy of God. He does not condemn those who ask for his mercy. Now pray with me. Will you pray with me?"

There was no answer. Henriette looked up from Cecile's cold hand into her eyes. They were still open, but unfocused now. Henriette spoke her name, but there was no response. Henriette knew from her almost daily experience of death that her dear and fragile sister had gone to God. Henriette laid her head on Cecile's folded hands and prayed, "Dear and gentle God, take her to your warm breast and hold her, for she is afraid. Let your holy face shine upon her and give her peace."

TWENTY-ONE

A few months after the funeral, Father Rousselon asked to see Henriette in his office. She came in her working clothes but wore white gloves.

"Are those white gloves in my honor?" Etienne said.

"Well, in a way. I have a bleeding rash on both hands, and the gloves cover up the bandages. They were a gift from Cecile."

"A rash? Have you seen a doctor?"

"Oh, it's nothing. The lye soap does it."

"I see," Etienne said, regarding her fondly. "And have they settled Cecile's estate?"

"Not yet. Mr. Hart's Austrian relatives are contesting her will. It seems that they want every penny."

"Who is representing your interests?"

"My brother, Jean, and his lawyer."

"I didn't know you had a brother."

"He lives in St. Martinsville. We are not close."

"Will Cecile's children live with Jean?"

"Probably. But it hasn't been decided yet."

"And what of Betsy?"

"Cecile left her to me. It is awkward."

"Do the Austrians want her, too?"

Henriette smiled. "It would serve them right. But we have talked, and Betsy will stay with the children."

"In the house on Burgundy Street?"

"I believe so. But Cecile left the house to Jean, and Jean and Betsy do not get along. So they will have to work it out."

"But you won't live there?"

"No. Betsy doesn't approve of my work among the slaves."

"But...she's a slave herself."

"Betsy doesn't think of herself as a slave."

"But, surely, you could occupy one floor?"

"No, no. Jean doesn't approve of my work either. No. I cannot live there."

"Ah," Etienne said, putting the fingers of both hands tip to tip. "Well, God does move in mysterious ways."

"I beg your pardon, Father?"

"You know, Henriette, that I have for some time been of the opinion that you and Josephine and Juliette should live together in community."

"Yes. We have talked of it."

"Well, I've been pursuing it. And I have found a house for rent, close by St. Augustine's, that I think would suit the purpose. It's run down, but the kitchen is in fairly good shape. There are four bedrooms, so that you could each have your own proper cell. It needs a front door, which I will see to, and the rent is nominal." Etienne sat back, obviously pleased with himself, and beamed at Henriette. "What do you say?"

"Why...why that's wonderful, Father. But the rent—I mean, I don't have a sou. None of us does."

"No wonder, after your wonderful contribution to the church fund."

"That was the money Maria gave me."

"Yes, you said that. But who is this Maria?"

"I believe you saw her at the shelter. That last day you came to anoint the slaves."

"Yes, I believe I did. The girl in the garish black dress?"

"She means well. It is a long story, Father, that I will tell you one day—if we decide to take her in as a postulant."

"Oh, I see."

"If she has any money left, which I doubt, because she has been so generous in buying supplies for the infirmary—if she has any money left, I'm sure she will offer it to defray the rent, at least in part." Henriette gave Etienne a definitive nod.

"It is not necessary. I've arranged with the bishop for the diocese to pay the rent until such time as you ladies can get established."

"Perhaps my inheritance. Once the thing is settled."

"And perhaps Father Pinchot can contribute a little."

"Oh, I don't think so, Father. He doesn't much like us."

"But he *is* coming around a bit, is he not?"

"Well, he is more available, yes. And he has lengthened his Mass to twenty-one minutes."

Etienne smiled. "I am glad to hear it. I was very hard with him in our last conversation."

"We heard you, Father. Clear out in the street. And we applauded you."

"Well, he has nothing to do with your new house."

"The new house." Henriette sat perfectly still, regarding Etienne with wide, dancing eyes. "Dear Jesus, is it possible?"

"Sweet Henriette. With your kind of faith anything is possible. Here." He wrote the address quickly on a piece of scrap paper and handed it to Henriette. "I'll meet you ladies out front shortly after Mass tomorrow morning. We'll look it over and see what has to be done."

Henriette leaned forward to take the note from Etienne's hand, fell forward to her knees, bowed her head, and prayed, "Oh dear good and holy Lord. A house of our own."

TWENTY TWO

The house was a shambles. The cobblestone courtyard was buckling underfoot, the plastered brick walls were crumbling, the iron gate hung on one hinge, and the house itself would long since have fallen down had it not been built of sturdy cypress planks. But the three women were delighted with it and, having swept it clean of trash and cobwebs, fell to whitewashing the front room and parlor for use as infirmaries. Three derelicts found living there had to be evicted because all were men, but a fourth — an ancient slave woman who spoke only a West African dialect — was received as their first patient and put in a newly whitewashed trundle bed in the parlor. She died on the third day, still bewildered and wide-eyed at the kindness of the ladies and the elegance of her rough muslin sheets.

By the time Brother Tobias had built and installed a new front door, the three women had moved into their rooms and had agreed upon a working version of the formal rule. Modeled on the Rule of St. Augustine — with which Henriette had become very familiar — it required that they would rise at 4:30 a.m. and retire at 9:30 p.m.; that they would meet three times a day (when feasible) for prayer and meditation; that they would share all things in common; and that they would form no liaisons or friendships without the knowledge and consent of all three. They proposed to make their living by laundering altar cloths and taking in the washing of religious and secular houses, and by public begging when necessary. They set no limit upon the number of patients they would take in, stating only they must be of the female sex and must agree, sooner rather than later, to receive some rudimentary instruction in the Catholic faith. They placed their faith in God, Bishop Blanc, and Father Rousselon, painted a small sign calling themselves by their new name, the Sisters of the Holy Family, which would allow them to function as a legal entity, and opened their new front door for God's business.

At the end of the first week, Betsy had a carter bring over a load of old blankets, sheets, china, pots, pans, and utensils from the house on Burgundy Street. She found Henriette and Brother Tobias out back, cleaning up the privy. Betsy, caustically frank as usual, rolled her eyes from the privy to the back of the sagging house, and said, "You mean to live in that, Miss Henriette?"

"Yes. Isn't it wonderful?"

"Well, that ain't the word that come to my mind."

"We have plenty of room for the indigents," Henriette said.

"Yes. Well, I brought you a bunch of old chamberpots and bedpans that I found in the attic."

"Oh, that's exactly what we need, Betsy."

"And somebody to empty them," said Brother Tobias, grinning at Betsy.

Betsy eyed him up and down coldly. "Looks to me like they's already got somebody." And, before Brother Tobias could answer, she turned to the carter and said, "What you standin' there for? Empty that stuff into the front room. I ain't got all day."

The next morning, Betsy told Henriette that Amelia Hart, one of Cecile's children, was feeling poorly and that Betsy felt she ought to stay on at the Burgundy Street house to care for her.

Henriette understood perfectly.

PART FOUR

1843–1847

❧ ETIENNE ❧

TWENTY-THREE

Friday

I have lately been preoccupied with slavery. If there is any practice under the sun that is more inimical to the health of the human spirit, I have no idea what it is. How can one man claim to *own* another man — own him body and soul, as if Almighty God had no dominion? Only God owns a soul, and therefore the body in which it inheres. And not even God presumes to control or in any way influence the sovereign self-determination of that soul or that body. God will infuse grace when it is devoutly and freely prayed for, but he will not interfere by so much as an impulse in the final disposition of any least second in the life of that soul, that body. We are *free* to go to hell if we like, and that freedom defines us, liberates us even from the benign will of God that all men should be saved. How dare a slave-owner arrogate unto himself powers that not even Almighty God chooses to exercise? Slavery is the absolute worst manifestation of man's defiance of God, and it poisons every aspect of a slave-owning society. Why is New Orleans considered to be so flagrantly decadent? I submit that it is largely because slavery is not only tolerated here, but it has been embraced, perversely, as one afflicted with a massive cancer might insanely watch its growth with pleasure and regard its ravages as just another unavoidable proceeding of natural law.

Whatever the religious or philosophical arguments on either side, I am most appalled by the everyday treatment of slaves. I have seen them whipped, truncheoned, beaten with chains and shackles — all quite publicly — and I have registered my protests on these occasions and have been told, more or less vulgarly, to go soak my head in holy water.

I have been rereading the work of my pamphleeter friend, the man with the fancy stickpin. And the more I see around me, the more I realize that he is mostly a reliable witness. Impassioned, yes, and constitutionally hyperbolic, but a man who does not flinch from the bloody truth.

He writes:

I have seen too much, and I have learned what I know, not from the idle tales of the demagogue nor the preaching of wild fanaticism, nor from what have been charged as the *embellished* stories of runaway slaves, but from having been an eyewitness, and having heard the groans and the shrieks of the mangled and bleeding slave, while being murdered under the lash and blows of the most inhuman of all monsters, the drivers and traffickers in human flesh.

Of the cruelties in the everyday mistreatment and murdering of slaves...I have never seen worse than I saw on a plantation a few miles above the city of New Orleans. I passed into the Negro yard and the first slave I met was grinding corn with a hand-mill like a common coffee grinder. He was chained to a post and was completely naked. A plank lay within reach of his chain, the *soft* side of which was his bed. His punishment was for running away, and he had been confined there to his mill seven weeks. In passing along to a shop, I found two Negroes working at blacksmithing. Both were chained to a block and were hampered with rings and chains on their legs. One of these was a stout mulatto man, and on his right ankle was a ring of iron studded with spikes. On the same leg near the knee was another such ring and a chain fastened from one ring to the other. The rings had worn and irritated the leg, and they were almost completely imbedded in the swollen flesh, so that from the knee to the top of the foot was one continuous putrid running sore. And yet he was at work preparing the heavy irons for a sugar mill. I asked him what he had those chains on for? He replied, "I run away, and by God I will again when I get these off and am well."

In passing toward the sugar field, I found a Negro sitting on a block. A physician from Mobile who was with me spoke to him, and as he raised his head a swarm of flies started off, and, looking on the right side of his head above the ear, I discovered the hair full of maggots, and the whole side was one mass of putrid matter. The skull was evidently broken in, as the matter which was running out indicated diseased bone.... He was perfectly conscious, yet did not answer questions, as he was clearly insane. And clearly dying, and not a thing to be done.

The "breakdown-whippings," as they are termed on the plantations, are usually done by placing the slave with his face to a post in which is framed a crossbar. An iron collar or ring is put round his neck and fastened to the post. The arms are extended each way and fastened to the crossbar by rings around the wrist. He is then stripped bare and whipped from twenty-five to fifty lashes and upward, sometimes as long as a man can continue to use the whip without being exhausted. Slaves often die there under the lash.

The whipping of women on plantations is in a different manner. Their frock is turned up over their head and they are made to lie down with the face to the ground, their arms extended and tied to a stake. A board is then taken which is prepared and shaped like a shovel. The wide part is bored full of small holes, and with this they are beaten on the bare flesh, from twenty-five to two hundred blows. After these blows are repeated a few times, the skin tears away, and the blood and flesh are forced through the holes in the board with great force and flies out into the air in dreadful red and white coils.

I sit here trembling. How can such things be? In the name of God, how?

But, in the name of God, why don't I do something about it?

Why don't I put aside my ecclesiastical offices and robes and go out in my shirt sleeves and join dear Henriette in what she has so bravely undertaken? What manner of man am I? I see the outrage, the injustice, the cancer upon the body politic, yet I satisfy myself with journal entries and pious murmurings! Dear God! Dear Henriette! I am sorry! I am truly sorry!

And, as for the slaves, the poor wretched slaves, they will judge me in the hereafter. I know it. And may they be flint-eyed and exacting. But I'm afraid that they won't. They are too sweet-natured and gentle, and they will say, "Oh, poor Father Rousselon, he did the best he could. You don't expect a high man of God to come down into the misery with the likes of us."

Dear God, what manner of priest am I? I know not. But whatever manner it is, certain it is that I am merely a man, and no least kind of martyr.

TWENTY-FOUR

Sunday

The ladies break my heart. They have scraped and scoured and whitewashed their house so that it literally glows. I blessed the house and consecrated the small brightwood altar (to be used only in emergencies), and they attended me as if I were the papal legate consecrating a side chapel at St. John Lateran. They are, the three of them, the most beautiful human souls I have ever encountered, and I cherish them. Brother Tobias, who has helped them significantly, and who built the altar, tries to maintain his distance from them, but I can see that he too has fallen under their spell. He cares no more than I do for their awful daily ministrations among the street slaves. But he worries about the women getting enough to eat. I have tried to persuade them that they should look to us for bare necessities, but Henriette is adamant: they will be self-sufficient, or else they will never be justified in calling themselves a religious order. How can I argue with that? And they do seem to have increased their laundering business to the point where they just might be self-sustaining.

I have to go on a tour of the working parishes in the course of this next month, and I am loath to leave my dear ladies in the hands of Father Pinchot. Antoine says he will keep an eye out for them, but Antoine has so many things to worry about that he might not attend them as carefully as they require, especially since Brother Tobias is going with me. The largest problem is that the sisters cannot be trusted to feed themselves properly. They may collect money from laundry from clients or realize a dollar or two from begging in the public squares, but those monies will disappear into the hands of the poor almost as soon as obtained. They seem to feel that money spent upon themselves, even to eat, is money wasted. Brother Tobias says that the only solution is to bring them food late in the evening, when they are off the streets and home for the Great Silence. Then they will eat, and Brother Tobias is often gone for a half-hour after the evening meal, bringing the women our leftovers. This kind of self-abnegation is rapidly disappearing from our society — and ought to be encouraged — but, dear God, the poor things will fast away to nothing unless they are carefully watched.

My tour of the outlying parishes is partly administrative, but also political. Antoine has in mind naming me as rector of the cathedral as of August 2, but we fully expect a fight. I don't look forward to it. The churchwardens claim that they alone have the right to name a rector. Antoine has started his own newspaper, *Le Propagateur Catholique*, to fight the churchwardens. It ought to be a very interesting summer.

Well, enough for now. I find I am growing more and more tried. Or, perhaps, bored is the word. We seem here so isolated from the heart of Holy Mother Church that, sometimes, I feel utterly useless and disenfranchised. I know this is unworthy of me and of my position as vicar-general, but, my dear Lord Jesus, the world out here is so raw and shrill and bumptious that I often feel just slightly ridiculous trying to represent a higher authority. These people are their own higher authority. So much so that I consider it a damned wonder that they managed to elect themselves a president.

I go too far. Bear with me, dear God. I shall one day learn to be a proper vicar of your church, and Peter's.

TWENTY-FIVE

Tuesday

I cannot believe what has just happened. I had no sooner arrived in Abbeville than the pastor, one of our oldest men, offered me a glass of wine. His name is Galuchet, and he is a very holy man, a simple man, whose smile lights up his face like a monstrance.

"I have been awaiting your visit, dear Father," he said, "so that I might share a glass or two of your marvelous largesse."

"Oh?" I said. "Largesse?"

"Why, yes. This splendid wine you sent me for my thirty-fifth anniversary as a priest."

"Why, of course," I said, assuming that Antoine had made one of his typical gestures. "I'd be delighted. I am parched."

Father Galuchet poured two glasses from a beautiful crystal decanter — which, he explained, was one of his prized possessions, a gift at his ordination — saying that the decanter had finally been fulfilled with a wine worthy of its beauty.

I did not suspect a thing until I sipped the wine — a great, robust, exquisite wine that seized the palate. The finest wine I had ever tasted... and, immediately, it came to me — Father Jacques Pinchot's cask!

"It is delicious, Father. It tastes to me like a...Romanée-Conti."

"You are exactly right!" He squinted at me. "But, surely, you knew...."

"No. I'm afraid Bishop Blanc made this choice." I lied, of course, but I was feeling my way. "You do still have the cask?"

"Oh, yes. I tapped it myself. I used to work at a winery in St. Estephe." He smiled. "You would like to see the cask?"

"Why, as matter of fact, I would."

"It's in the cellar, under the summer kitchen. Come, I'll show you."

I was mainly interested to see how much was left in the cask but also, if possible, to discover how it had been addressed, how, of all of Father Pinchot's paraphernalia, it alone had gone astray.

Father Galuchet addressed the first as we started down into the low-ceilinged cellar. "I'm afraid there isn't much left. Perhaps a half-gallon or so. I had relatives visiting me from France this spring, and well, they had to be restrained. I had to hide the cask under the potatoes."

The second perplex was addressed and answered as soon as I saw the cask. It had been scorched into almost entire blackness with only the words "Romanée-Conti" barely legible above the spigot.

"What on earth?" I said.

"Oh, I forgot. The drayman's cart was struck by lightning. Burned up most of his carload. Only some minor heroics on his part saved the cask. A true Frenchman. He kicked the burning crate off the cask and rolled it into the swamp. I rewarded him with a quart of the wine. I must say, I think the flames improved the taste of it, if anything. A truly amiable act of God."

I stared at the man, blinking. But I could discern no guilt in him, no least hint of deception. He truly believed that the bishop had spent well over a thousand dollars rewarding him for his priestly fidelity. What could I say? Could I destroy his pleasure, his beatific — if slightly tipsy — pleasure in his gift? No. Not I.

I examined the cask. "Well, no question but that it is Romanée-Conti." I said. "And thank God they use sturdy French oak casks."

"Oh, yes, yes," he said. "I wrote them a letter congratulating them on their prescience. But I haven't heard back yet."

"Did you ever write to the bishop?"

"Why, of course. I thanked him for the splendid commemoration of my anniversary."

I remembered seeing such a letter, but, since there had been no mention of a cask of wine, I assumed the usual: that the bishop had said a Mass in his honor or some such.

"I've been meaning to write him, now that I've tasted the wine, to tell him how fine it is. I'll get to it today."

"Yes, do that. The bishop will be pleased."

When I got back to New Orleans, I immediately went to see Father Pinchot. I had every intention of telling him about his cask, but he received me in such a supercilious manner that I changed my mind.

"Well," he said, grinning at me over a glass of Pernod and water. "The father of us all."

"You're drunk, Father."

"No, but I am working on it. Your ladies put me through a hideous afternoon. We buried at least two slaves, maybe three. It is hard to remember. But they are safely in the ground and in God's hands, and I am attempting to recuperate."

"You feel put upon?"

"No, Father. I feel entombed."

"Your self-pity is dismaying."

"Oh, don't be dismayed, Father. I shall rise again. Just as soon as I can get around to describing my situation to the Vatican."

"You'd do that?"

"Well, it is the preferable option to suicide."

"Father Pinchot, if you really are so dreadfully bent upon leaving your mission, I can arrange your departure posthaste."

"Of course, Father, of course. But that wouldn't bring me, or my case, to the attention of the cardinal in charge of outrages, now would it?"

"I have a strong feeling that your route to the attention of the cardinal in charge of outrages will take quite another course, if you don't straighten yourself out. And soon."

"Oh, dreary dear. Is that a threat?"

"Take it as you like, Father. You are in too pitiable a state for me to attempt to elaborate."

I turned and started for the door. "Is that it?" he said. "Is that what you came for?"

I turned. "No. I came to tell you that your cask of wine is no more. It has found a better home than you could possibly have given it."

"Oh, really." He lifted his glass. "Well, then, give my compliments to the bishop. And convey my congratulations upon his splendid taste in rare vintages."

"I'll do that," I said, thoroughly sick of the man. "And you give my regards to Bacchus."

I went out, appalled. Yet I knew that Antoine would be delighted with the disposition of the cask and the nice misunderstanding as to its final resting place.

❧ HENRIETTE ❧

TWENTY-SIX

She had to carry the poor woman the last fifty yards in a driving rain. The new girl, Apoline, opened the door, and started to scream, "She's daid! That one's daid!"

"Be quiet, Apoline," Henriette said, "and go make up the spare bed."

"Yes, sister, but she's daid! Bad, bad luck!"

Henriette set the woman on a towel on the floor of the small lavatory and washed her head to toe with a washcloth and lye soap. The woman was tiny — under five feet tall — and she watched Henriette out of large eyes full of fear and wonderment. When Henriette brought her in to the bed and covered her with the heavy sheets and a threadbare blanket, she said her first words: "May him bless you."

"Do you mean God?" Henriette said.

"Yes'm. God bless."

"She ain't daid?" Apoline said from the doorway.

"Is there anything to eat in the house?" Henriette asked.

"Just some of that punkin soup."

"Put it on the stove."

"But that's our own supper, Miss Henriette."

"Heat it up, Apoline. This woman needs it more than we do."

"Ain't got but two pieces of wood left."

"Use them."

"Yes, ma'am."

Apoline disappeared toward the kitchen, and Henriette got out her small medical kit and began to treat the woman's sores with alcohol. There was one sore, down below her belly button, that was the size of a crabapple and suppurating. Henriette cleaned it, but it immediately filled with pus again.

"This isn't a plague sore, is it?" she asked the woman.

"Don't know. Been there a little while."

"How long?"

"Oh, three, four weeks."

"Well, I think if it were the plague, it would have killed you by now."

"Oh, it'll kill me," the woman said softly. "Bye and bye."

"You get her outta here," Apoline said.

Henriette turned. Apoline was standing at the door with the kitchen knife in her hand. "Apoline, what are you doing with our knife?"

"She ain't stayin' here. She got the 'bonics plague. Just like you said."

Henriette got to her feet and walked over to Apoline. "Give me the knife, Apoline. You don't know what you're saying." Apoline backed away, into the hallway. "You stay away now! I don't want to hurt nobody, but I will."

"Apoline, you do not run this house. I do. Now give me that knife this minute!"

As Henriette started toward her, her hand out for the knife, Apoline turned and ran into the kitchen, shouting, "I don't wanna kill nobody! But I got me a curse! A evil curse! Don't come near me!"

Henriette stood staring. What in God's name had they admitted into their midst? Apoline had appeared on the doorstep less than a week ago, saying that she wanted to save her soul and join the women. She said she was from out toward Natchitoches, that she was a free Creole, and that she had five dollars dowry money to give to Henriette and the others. Juliette was suspicious from the beginning, especially when it appeared that she'd sewn the five dollars into her dress and now couldn't find where. She was wearing a nice dress that fit her reasonably well, but she had feet too big for her shoes, and, as Juliette said, "had the hands and shoulders of a field hand." She was carrying a carpetbag, which she kept very close to her, and said that her education had been neglected because her parents had split up and left her with an ancient grandmother who had recently died.

Henriette had her suspicions, but Apoline seemed like a nice enough sixteen-year-old and should be given the benefit of any doubt. She had come a long way to see them, was well enough spoken, well enough dressed, and was quite probably exactly who she said she was. They had given her the small attic room, had told her she might become a full-fledged community member in six months, and welcomed her strong back into the community.

Up until today, she had worked hard and given no reason for concern. Now Henriette stood in the hallway wondering what she could safely do. There were two patients in the room behind her. She must not allow Apoline to get past her and into the patients' room with that knife. And there was another door off the lavatory. She went into the patients' room, closed the other door, and pushed one of the beds up against it, all the time being watched by both patients, their eyes wide and quick.

Then she returned to the hallway, blessed herself, and walked briskly into the kitchen. Apoline was standing with her back to the pantry door, still holding the knife in front of her.

Henriette crossed to Apoline and stopped about four feet from her as Apoline extended the knife.

"I'll cut you," Apoline said.

"Why would you do that, Apoline?"

"You keep bringin' daid people in here."

"They aren't dead."

"They dyin'!"

"Would you deny them a last few hours of relative comfort?"

"I ain't no relative!"

"You're their sister in Christ."

"Don't you say that! I cut you! They ain't no kin of mine!"

"No, they're not. In the flesh. But in the spirit, they are."

"No, they ain't!" And Apoline took a broad swing with the knife.

Henriette stepped back quickly, and the knife missed her by a good two feet. Apparently, she thought, Apoline didn't really want to hurt her. "You are being very foolish, Apoline. You say you have a curse on you. Why don't you tell me what it is and we will deal with it together."

"Nothin' you can do. It's a voodoo curse. I got a gris-gris put on me!"

"Where is this gris-gris?"

"I throwed it away from me! What do you think? But it got its curse on me anyways!"

"Will you kneel down and pray with me? I'm sure if we ask the Blessed Virgin for help, she will intercede on your behalf."

"Don't you hear me? It's a voodoo! Ain't nobody can fix it but a voodoo."

"Well, then," Henriette said, "well, then, perhaps we ought to go see Marie Laveau."

"Marie Laveau! You know Marie Laveau?"

"It happens we are distantly related, and I know her well enough to ask a favor."

"You believe in voodoo?"

"No, I don't. But that you apparently do is all that matters. She lives over on Dumaine just off of Bourbon Street. We can be there within half an hour."

"I don't know," Apoline said. "She the voodoo queen. She just might strike me dead."

"I assure you that won't happen," Henriette said. "Now give me the knife, and come along."

"I don't know," Apoline said. But she lowered the knife and eased it gently toward Henriette. When it could be easily reached, Henriette took it by the blade.

"Now," she said, "the sun is out, the patients will be safe enough for an hour or so. Get your hat, and we'll go."

"Yes, ma'am." Apoline said, suddenly chastened. "You sure she won't strike me dead?"

"Quite sure. Get your hat."

Apoline turned to the attic stairs and ran up them. Henriette heaved a great sigh of relief, walked over to the back door, stepped outside, pushed the knife into the ground about half its length, and broke the blade off just below the handle before throwing the remains over the back fence into the swamp. She was saying a prayer to St. Teresa of Avila as she came back into the kitchen.

Apoline came thumping down the narrow stairs, holding her hat in place and carrying her bag. She looked at Henriette closely. "You goin' to do what you said, now?"

"Right now," Henriette said, and moved off toward the front door.

They found Marie Laveau in her front yard clipping her rose bushes. Now perhaps fifty, she looked thirty or younger, and her legendary beauty was still evident. She turned as Henriette approached, smiling and nodding. "Well, Henriette, you honor my house."

"Thank you, Marie. I'm afraid I have brought you some trouble."

Marie looked past Henriette to Apoline, who was standing with her hands folded, looking utterly terrified. "That one?" Marie asked.

"Yes. She insists there is a voodoo curse upon her."

"My God," Marie said. "Who would bother?" But she smiled quickly at Henriette. "I will handle it, my dear. You go on home. I'll send her to you when I'm done." Henriette nodded, and Marie said, "You do want to see her again?"

Henriette hesitated. "I would rather not."

"Then I'll take care of that, too. Go in peace."

"Thank you, Marie. I shall pray for you."

"Thank you, Henriette. It isn't often that I have a saint praying for me."

Henriette blushed, bowed her head to the compliment, and left the garden. As she passed Apoline, she could see that the poor girl was stricken, still as a stone.

Juliette, candle in one hand, drew the blade from the mud outside the kitchen door. "That's the only knife we have for the kitchen," she said.

"I'm sorry, Juliette," she said. "But I was that frightened."

"Oh, I'm sure you were, my dear," said Josephine.

"I wish I'd been here," Juliette said. "I'd have shown her how we deal with knife-wielders in Cuba."

"Why wasn't Maria here?" Josephine asked.

"She went to beg at the cathedral. I'm glad she didn't see it. It would have upset her terribly."

"We don't expect Apoline back?" Juliette asked.

"No, no," Henriette said. "She's not stable."

"Should we offer her room to Maria? She must be getting tired of that rooming house."

"Well, we might. She won't be back here tonight, so perhaps we'll talk to her in the morning. If we are all agreed."

"I am in favor," Josephine said. Juliette nodded.

"Good." Then, to Josephine. "Did you bring some wine for our ceremony?"

"No. I had no money." She turned to Juliette. "I thought you might, with the money from St. Patrick's."

"St. Patrick's," Juliette said sourly, "says they will pay up the whole laundry and altar cloth bill on Monday next. So I had no money either."

"No matter," Henriette said. "We will make do."

The women inspected the pantry, the cupboards, and the ice box, and found them all empty.

"Apoline," Henriette said. "She must have taken it all in her carpetbag. Not that there was that much."

"Well, here's a bit of sugar she missed," Juliette said.

"That will do just fine," Henriette said.

And so the three women raised their glasses of sugared water fervently and hopefully, looking forward to that time when the See of Rome should decide to declare them well-found and welcome. At the very end, when they were all on their knees in front of the small kitchen shrine, Henriette raised a final prayer.

"Dear Jesus, Mary, and Joseph, we are your poorest servants, we are the servants of slaves. What we offer you in our committed poverty is our determination to bring the abject poor — newly cleansed and chastised — into the pure holiness of the Kingdom. And to do this without stint until we ourselves have worn out our bodies and can present our wretched souls, penitent, for the scrutiny of your holy eyes. Until then, we, the lowliest of the holy Catholic company, pledge unto you our faith, our flesh, and the very bones and marrow of our beings. And we ask only that you place our poor cause before the throne of God and ask his mercy upon it."

All three said "Amen," got to their feet, and embraced. They went to their straw beds, their bellies empty but their hearts full of joy.

❧ ETIENNE ❧

TWENTY-SEVEN

Thursday

I dreamed again last night of Canigou. Of the ragged granite ramparts and the high blue windless skies of the Pyrenées Orientales up on the Spanish border. My Uncle Albert and I would disembark at Avignon and take a coach to Carcassonne, stay overnight, and then rent a private vehicle for the trip up into the mountains of Roussillon Province. Near the end, the roads would become so narrow and rough, barely clinging to the mountainsides, that the driver had to get down and lead the horses around the rock-ribbed bends. Uncle Albert would let me ride outside, up on the high seat with the driver, and I would always be the first to spot the towers of the monastery. Saint-Martin-du-Canigou, built by the Benedictines in 1001, was then and forever my Camelot, my Xanadu.

Uncle Albert would stock up on wine in Avignon — the *vin d'Avignon* (the incipient Chateauneuf-du-Pape) — and in Carcassonne with Côte du Roussillon-Villages. And he knew a butcher in Carcassonne who rounded up the finest duck, chicken, loin of lamb and beef, ham, and suckling pig every year upon notice from Uncle Albert, and would have them packed in barrels and crates for transport up to the monastery. Nor did he neglect ports, sherries, candies, and other sweets, so that our arrival at the monastery was always cause for celebration, if not jubilation, as the abbot and forty smiling monks surrounded us and unloaded the wagon into the refectory.

Uncle Albert and the abbot had been novices together forty years before at Canigou, but if anyone — least of all Uncle Albert — regretted his failure to make it as a Benedictine, it was certainly not apparent. We were treated like royalty, and the three or four days we spent there were joyous and celebratory in the truest Benedictine sense. Benedict said that the visitor should be treated as if Christ himself had come to call, and there was no smallest stint in the reception we always received.

And the dinners! Prepared by Brother Leopold, who had once been a chef at a famous restaurant in Lyon, the dinners were works of art. For the first two or three nights, dinner was a small, private affair, hosted by the abbot and his immediate staff. But on the final night of our stay, the dinner was open to all of the monks — served in the great refectory — with wine, sweets, and port available to all. And while the monks were temperate and perfectly well behaved, the atmosphere was electric, full of Christian joy and love, and when we went in to vespers and compline, the chanting was gloriously full and sonorous and rolled around the stones of the vaulted main church like the sound of men who had the ear of God and, by God, meant to hold it.

Why I didn't become a Benedictine is a long story involving my mother's friendship with the bishop of Lyon and my father's great disappointment that I was going to become a priest — let alone a cloistered monk — so acute a disappointment that I felt he never really forgave me. He was an atheist to the very end and died saying that, if there was a God, he would have a few thousand things to say to him about the pain and evil in the world. I flatter myself sometimes into thinking that I may just by now have prayed him out of purgatory, but it is not at all something I therefore neglect. I would not, in fact, be surprised if, after the twelve years since his death, he has gotten finished with his conversation with God.

I not only dream about Canigou, I often think about it. Especially when I feel myself beleaguered by all of the thousand things of my vicar-generalship. I imagine what a blissful existence life as a Benedictine at Saint-Martin-du-Canigou might have been. The sweetness of the liturgy, the chanting of the Divine Office, the communion with God in that pure and holy air. But it was, obviously, not my true calling. And think of all I would have missed. Coming to the

New World, taking on its enormous spiritual problems, feeling the exaltation of the missionary, getting to know Antoine.

But most especially, getting to know Henriette Delille. And the knowledge that there is true, courageous sanctity in this world, bravery that far exceeds that which it takes for a monk to rise in the middle of a cold winter's night to sing the divine praises. Pray on, dear monks, but never think you have the grail cornered and unto yourselves. For I could show you muddy corners of the streets of New Orleans that, when she passes, glow with a holiness that would make you turn your eyes away.

TWENTY EIGHT

Saturday

Some time ago, Henriette asked me if there might be, in the convent library, a life of St. Teresa of Jesus, better known as St. Teresa of Avila. She had heard of the book from an Ursuline nun, who was quite certain that there was one available in the rare books section of the Great Convent's library. I went in search and finally found it. The book was in remarkably good shape and, as soon as I put it in Henriette's hands — and saw the reverence with which she received it — I knew the exhausting search in the cold and dark reaches of the library had been worth the effort.

She returned the book to me today, in perfect shape, and said that it had been inspiring, beautiful, yet very practical in its spiritual discussions. She talked about the saint's life and found some parallels with her own, but concluded that she could never possibly achieve such holiness. I hope St. Teresa was listening.

She said that she was very touched by the poem "The Flaming Hart," which was dedicated "Upon the book and picture of the seraphical St. Teresa." I said that I hadn't noticed the poem, whereupon she recited it to me.

O thou undaunted daughter of desires!
By all thy dowr of Lights and Fires;
By all the eagle in thee, all the dove;
By all thy lives and deaths of love;
By thy large draughts of intellectuall day,
And by thy thirsts of love more large than they;
By all thy brim-fill'd Bowles of fierce desire;
By thy last Morning's draught of liquid fire;
By the full kingdome of that finall kisse
That seiz'd thy parting Soul, and seal'd thee his;
By all the heavn's thou hast in him
(Fair sister of the Seraphim!);
By all of Him we have in Thee;
Leave nothing of my Self in me.
Let me so read thy life, that I
Unto all life of mine may dy.

She recited with such intense love and holy precision that I was dumbstruck for a moment or two. She seemed to have transfixed herself in God's light while she sat before me. I had to blink despite myself, and I told her I would copy out the poem so she might have it for her prayers. She said that wouldn't be necessary; she had it by heart forever. (I copied it out anyway, for my own sake.)

Then, much to my astound, she told me that her great-great grandfather, Claude Joseph Dubreuil, had built this convent. Dubreuil was the royal engineer, contractor of the king of France, and one of colonial Louisiana's most prosperous plantation owners. He was responsible for designing and constructing most of Louisiana's levee and canal works. Henriette said that Dubreuil owned her great-great grandmother, Marie Ann, a slave woman brought from Africa in the ships, and that he, Claude Joseph Dubreuil, fathered upon her three children: Marie Ann, Cecile, and Etienne. Dubreuil did not free Marie Ann or her children before he died. One of his sons, Claude Joseph Dubreuil, Jr., freed them more than ten years after his father's death. The children took their father's surname, Dubreuil, when they were freed, and it was Cecile Dubreuil who was Henriette's great-grandmother. Henriette's brother and sister knew who their fathers were, as did Henriette, but her father took no interest in her welfare.

She finished this recital in a small voice, and my heart went out to her.

"That must be very hard on you, harder when you were a child, not to know your father."

"Yes. I pray for him often."

I nodded. I could see the subject was very painful to her, so I went on to something else. "That group of lay women you organized — how is it doing?"

"We call it the Association of the Holy Family. It is doing quite well. We have medical supplies now. And none of us goes hungry."

"Excellent."

"I have appointed Madame Cecilia Deouay as president, and, with your approval, I would like to turn the leadership over to her."

"Of course. She is a considerable lady."

"Yes. She wants to buy a plot over on St. Bernard Avenue and build a home for the elderly. I have already written the letter for permission. You should have it as soon as we have all signed it."

"I'll be delighted to approve it. And I'm sure the bishop will agree. Will you be moving then?"

"Yes, I think so. There is a small house. We will add on to it for the hospice."

"Forgive me, but you don't seem very enthusiastic."

"Well, a home for the elderly is a very good thing, but it isn't what we've been doing. I mean, our slave women from the streets are not merely elderly. And we must not neglect them."

"Of course not." I studied her for a moment. She looked drawn, tired, but the inner flame was still strong, undiminished. "Have you any new members?" I asked.

"No," she said. "And I feel that we won't have until we can find a proper house. My dear sister Cecile has left me some money, I understand. When I get it, I will start looking for a house. One with room for new members. Then I am sure more will come."

"That will go a long way toward getting you recognized officially as an order."

"Yes, but we have so much to learn. If we could only enter a convent for a few months, we could see how things are done. How proper nuns go about their lives."

"You mean that? You would take the time?"

"With all my heart."

"Well, let me look into it. See what can be done."

"Oh, I've hesitated to ask. But if you could find something. . . . "

A smile, and a beatific eagerness in her eyes. And it was still there, shining, when she took her leave. I sat down immediately and started a letter to the mother superior of St. Michael's Convent, in Convent, Louisiana. It would not be easy, but a truly zealous vicar-general can accomplish amazing things when he applies himself.

PART FIVE

1848–1852

❧ HENRIETTE ❧

TWENTY-NINE

The home for the elderly proved to be nothing to Henriette's specific purpose. The women admitted were mostly friends or even the mothers of the members of the Association of the Holy Family. They were neither indigent nor in particularly dire physical straits and were uniformly horrified when Henriette and Josephine carried in their first slave victim from the streets. Arrangements were hurriedly made to isolate the poor slave woman from the others, but there wasn't much that could be immediately done about the stench, and this was protested even after the poor woman, who died the first night, had been carried out and buried by Henriette and Charles.

The three women got together after Mass the next morning. "It won't do," Juliette said. "What we're running is a nursing home."

"That isn't what we set out to do," Josephine said. "They should hire a cook and a nurse. And we should go about our business."

"I agree," said Henriette. "But we have made a commitment, and I'm afraid we must honor it until we can gently persuade them to fend for themselves. Meanwhile I shall start looking for another house. I finally have my inheritance, and it will certainly do for a beginning."

"I think I know where I can find a cook," Juliette said.

"Good," said Henriette. "But the residents are dear ladies, and we must not be too abrupt."

The dear ladies solved the problem. When the three women and Maria got back to the house, they found that the ladies had bowed to the wishes of the church parish trustees and had admitted a young man severely stabbed by a gambler. Henriette treated his wounds but forthwith informed the ladies that neither she nor her companions could remain under the same roof with a man, as it would create scandal. So, over howling protests and apologies, Henriette, Josephine, Juliette, and Maria — directly after serving lunch — packed up their things and departed.

They stayed the first night with Betsy, who had so much room she was thinking of taking in a boarder.

Betsy took a long look at the foursome. "You don't look so good," she said. "And you stink like dead bodies."

"Then we will clean ourselves up," Henriette said. And the four went upstairs and did so. Betsy found black dresses, which had belonged to Cecile, for Henriette, Josephine, and Maria. And she gave Juliette one of her own. While the four ladies were bathing and scrubbing, Betsy boiled their old clothes and their shoes. None of the latter survived, but substitutes were found, and they all sat down to a jambalaya while Betsy railed at them about living like a bunch of white trash and surely "ruining" their lives.

"I'd have you come live here, take good care of you if you'd only stop collectin' dead bodies off the streets and bringin' them home!"

"Now, Betsy, you know better. They aren't dead bodies," Henriette said.

"Next thing to it," Betsy said,

"Betsy, don't you understand?" Henriette said. "We baptize them, give them the means to go to heaven. Often we can find a priest to give them the last rites."

"Slaves got no rights," Betsy said. "No heaven for slaves."

"Well, of course there is, Betsy," Henriette said softly. "You will go to heaven whether you want to or not."

Within a few days, Henriette had found and purchased a house at 72 Bayou Road. It needed repairs, so they moved into a rental house on Chartres Street near the Great Convent while the repairs were being made.

And it was here that the immense effort and strain of the past dozen years began to catch up with Henriette. She fell ill—very seriously ill—and had to take to her bed. The doctor, a great, gentle man by the name of Verdet, examined her carefully and told Josephine and Juliette that she was near death by exhaustion. The only treatment was rest, a very long and complete rest.

But it was a hot spring heading into an even hotter summer, and opportunities for rest were fitful at best. Convinced that she was dying, Henriette summoned M. Octave de Armas, a notary, and dictated her will. She bequeathed the house on Bayou Road to Antoine Blanc and his successors for the purpose of continuing the work of the Sisters of the Holy Family, "having for its object the religious instruction of the poor and illiterate."

She bequeathed Betsy to her seldom-seen brother, Jean. That she owned a slave had long bothered her, and her thought had always been to give Betsy her freedom. But Betsy had resisted, and by 1850 the laws of Louisiana governing the freeing of slaves had become quite complicated. In order to free Betsy, Henriette would have had to post a large bond, and Betsy would be obliged to leave the state. The state was concerned that, if too many slaves were freed in Louisiana, stayed there, and began to congregate, uprisings and slave revolts might result. So the simple fact was that Betsy did not want to be freed if it meant having to leave Henriette and her friends and family.

Henriette bequeathed her movable goods to her dear friend Juliette and her rosary to Father Rousselon, and then she lay back and prepared to depart this world.

But she recovered. While her companions in Christ, her family, her friends, Betsy and Charles, and even some of the street people rejoiced, she heaved herself out of her bed, knelt to Father

Rousselon's blessing, and arose to take up the cudgels and resume the work of her Sovereign Christ.

THIRTY

By the end of 1852, the small community was established in the house at 72 Bayou Road. The women had received a new member, Magdaleine Chaigneauy — a devout young woman who showed distinct promise.

So did the new house. It had seven rooms: a large kitchen, parlor, and bedroom downstairs, and four bedrooms upstairs. The parlor became the infirmary, and the workmen had found a large wooden watering trough that served as a bathtub for the patients. The workmen had even bored a hole in the trough and arranged a fairly efficient drainage system and had also provided two sturdy oaken buckets for fetching the bath water. All of it, with a new roof, some new flooring, and a heavy front door with bars had cost Henriette less than forty dollars of her inheritance. She considered the money very well spent, for with its three fireplaces, a wood stove in the kitchen, and a good well, the place was the fulfillment of the great dream: a proper house in which to live and conduct God's business.

But the community had barely settled in when Henriette received a summons from Father Rousselon to meet with him and the archbishop at the Great Convent. Henriette was apprehensive. She had not spoken to Antoine Blanc since his investiture as archbishop on February 16, 1851. This was in accordance with a papal bull issued on July 19, 1850, by Pope Pius IX, establishing the Archdiocese of New Orleans, which as a Metropolitan Province was to include the Suffragan Sees of Galveston (the whole state of Texas), Little Rock (the state of Arkansas), Natchez (the state of Mississippi), and Mobile (the state of Alabama). Henriette, who knew her geography, was amazed by the sheer size of the thing, and her respect for Antoine Blanc was commensurately magnified. She put on her best dress and shoes and went up to the residence praying to God that the great man had not lost patience with the trifling efforts of her little band of sisters.

Father Rousselon received her with a warm smile and ushered her directly into the presence of the archbishop. He rose to greet her and said, "Well, Miss Delille, I think we have some good news for you."

Henriette almost collapsed with relief. She bent to kiss the archbishop's ring, and he took her gently by the arms and eased her into one of the chairs in front of the desk. Then he took his own chair behind the desk, smiled at her, and waved Father Rousselon into the other chair.

"Well, Father Rousselon told me of your wish to get some formal training at a convent, with an eye toward getting your little order correctly established."

"Yes, I—"

"Why then," he interrupted, "as you may know, I am on extremely good terms with the Madames of the Sacred Heart. In fact, whenever I feel the need of an escape from my episcopal duties, I flee to St. James Parish to spend a few days as a guest of the sisters. They run St. Michael's School for young ladies, and I must say the food is exceptionally good."

"I am, very pleased—"

"So that I had no hesitation, when Father Rousselon told me he had written to Mother Praz with your petition, to intercede directly with her in your behalf. And I am delighted to tell you that she graciously acceded to our request."

"Oh, thank you! I scarcely—"

"She can only take two of you at a time, if that's all right with you."

"Why that's exactly—you see, someone has to stay behind, so Josephine can tend to the house while Juliette and I—"

"It's settled then. You work out the details with Father Rousselon, and let me give my blessing to the enterprise." He got to his feet, blessed her as she scrambled to her knees, smiled hugely, and brought his hands together in a great clap. "You'll excuse me, Etienne. I have to speak to the churchwardens." And out he went.

Father Rousselon beamed at her. "So? The cause proceeds."

"Oh, thank you, Father. Thank God."

"Yes, thank God. But also thanks to you, Henriette." He rose, offered his hand, and helped her to her feet. "You and your little ladies have brought a holiness to New Orleans that it would otherwise not obtain. We are edified by your works and by your presence. You know that."

Henriette stood and then bowed her head and fell to one knee. "Your blessing, Father."

Father Rousselon gave her the most formal of blessings. "Dear Henriette," he said. "I will miss you while you are away, but you will be remembered first in every Mass I say, every single morning."

She looked at him with such love and thanksgiving in her eyes that he almost looked away. Then she took his hand, kissed it, and walked rapidly from the room.

And if, as they say, a heart can sing, Henriette's lifted a motet in four-part harmony all the way home.

THIRTY-ONE

Mother Annette Praz, superior of the St. Michael's community of the Madames of the Sacred Heart, was a tall, plain woman with an air of implacability. She sat looking across her tidy desk at Henriette and Juliette, with an expression of amusement on her otherwise inscrutable face.

"So, Miss Delille, Miss Gaudin, you are very highly thought of by the archbishop and Father Rousselon."

There was a moment of silence. Then Henriette said, "We are pleased to hear this. We certainly think very highly of them."

"Well, I daresay" — she took in a deep breath and exhaled — "I understand Father Rousselon's effusive letter, you are both free women of color, and you are bent upon establishing an order of colored nuns in New Orleans."

Another moment. "You are exactly right in that, Mother Praz," Henriette replied.

"I see," Mother Praz said, nodding her head. "And do you think this is a truly feasible undertaking? Or are you simply testing the waters for, shall I say, those who will come after you?"

Absolutely not," Henriette said. "We are determined to bring it about in our time, and under the auspices of our dear Father Rousselon and our beloved Archbishop Blanc."

Mother Praz blinked and regarded Henriette with a chastened eye. "You express yourself very forcefully, my child." She looked from Henriette to Josephine and back again. "May I say something that you may find quite out of order?"

"Of course, Mother," Henriette said. "But I am certain we will find it completely in order."

Mother Praz rearranged herself in her great high-backed chair, and relaxed her mouth into something like a smile. "You are both quite comely young women, and you are both so . . . well, may I say it, nearly *white* that you could have, as they say, passed almost anywhere. Certainly in this order." She cocked her head at them, smiling a quite friendly smile. "Why haven't you at least tried?"

Henriette paused and looked at Juliette, who gave Henriette a small nod. "Because," Henriette said, "that would have been wholly contrary to our purpose. We are black, however partially, and we are not ashamed of it. We are humble but whole before the Lord who made us. And what we wish to do is to give the black woman in Louisiana a clear choice between concubinage and the holy service of the Lord, our God,"

Mother Praz's stiff features twitched with surprise. She opened her mouth to speak and closed it again. Then, very quietly, she said, "I feel like applauding. But I will leave that for the angels."

"You are too kind," Henriette said.

"And you," she said to Juliette. "Does Henriette always speak for you?"

"We are of a mind," Juliette said softly. "And she speaks so much better than I."

Mother Praz looked from one to the other and back again. "I'm going to have to assign you two to the scullery. I have to honor the customs of this house. I hope you understand."

"Dear Mother," said Henriette, "the scullery will be like heaven to us."

Mother Praz regarded them in silence for a moment. Then she spoke slowly and solemnly. "This house is honored by your presence." She sat perfectly still in the following silence and then suddenly stood and clapped her hands softly together. "I will be right back."

Henriette looking at Juliette. "Do you believe this is happening?"

"Not yet. But I feel God's love strongly in this house."

"So do I. St. Michael is here."

"Does he have his broadsword?"

"Why, I'm sure he does. Why do you ask?"

"Onions and potatoes. He needn't use his broadsword. We could loan him a paring knife."

"Juliette!" Henriette said. Then she started to giggle and both were still giggling then Mother Praz came marching back into the room.

She stopped short, looking at them. "Is there something funny?"

"Oh," said Henriette, "it was a silly thing."

Mother Praz looked at them sternly. "There is nothing laughable here, ladies. Think of Jesus on his cross, and what seems laughable will soon take its perspective."

"Yes, Mother," Henriette said. "It will not happen again." Mother Praz looked at her for a moment and nodded. "Now, stand up, and I'll show you to your quarters."

THIRTY-TWO

The first shock was the cleanliness of everything. Henriette and Juliette had been brought up in formal households, and they had known cleanliness before as a way of life; they had once worn crinolines starched white and stiff as altar cloths. But their years in the service of slaves had somewhat blunted their requirements, had even dimmed their memories of what it was like to be free of the mud and the blood, the stench and the pus, the awful aroma of the dead and dying, and the constant exhaustion that made them lie down to sleep unclean, with the dirt caked about their ankles and bloody spittle still staining their patched dresses.

To be suddenly free of these abominations was stunning, and they came into the first days of their visit like two young soldiers, fresh off some battlefield, laid down in clean sheets washed and sweet smelling, their senses singing with the redemption of it all. To rise in the night to attend matins and to listen to the choir nuns chanting the Divine Office seemed to them the highest of privileges. When they were asked by the mistress of novices if they found rising in the night offices irksome, they looked astonished, and Henriette said, "Dear Lord, no. There's no one dead or dying, no one to bury." The mistress of novices, wide-eyed, said, "Oh, I see," and moved quickly away.

The food was a bit of a problem. Though suitably spartan, the convent food was far too rich for Henriette and Juliette. Rich and heavily spiced. They were not so far away from their dinners of sugared water, and, after dutifully eating normal portions of a Cajun-flavored chicken gumbo, they became thoroughly sick to their stomachs, lost their dinners, and lost most of their interest in eating at all. They confined themselves to bread, butter, milk, eggs, and a lot of water for the first few weeks of their stay at the convent.

The simple clothing they had been given was, of course, not the normal habits given to novices. That would have been a violation of the rules of the house and the order, as black women were not permitted to wear the full habit. Henriette and Juliette made do with simple white muslin dresses gathered at the middle by a short length of rope and with white headpieces rather like maid's caps. They were also given light shawls for the cooler mornings and shoes from the common collection of the nuns.

Their duties in the scullery were mostly confined to peeling, slicing, and dicing, the washing of pots, dishware, and tableware, and the setting of the refectory tables. They enjoyed the work so much that they felt somewhat guilty about it and used whatever "spare" time they had assisting the infirmarian with washing linens, boiling and rolling bandages, and keeping the bedpans empty and sparkling clean. They became known in the infirmary as "our colored angels," but Mother Praz said, "You don't treat angels like scullion drudges." She brought their exploitation to an end by forbidding them to work in the infirmary.

Yet they were happy, and they adjusted to the convent routine with great ease. Sometimes they discussed how they would have a convent of their own one day, devoted to their mission among the slaves but equally devoted to the recruitment and training of black women in the religious life. Henriette's eyes would glow with intensity, and she would say, "God cannot have brought us this far without intending that we succeed. Let us pray, Juliette, pray every minute and make ourselves holy."

They did, and it was noticed. Mother Praz eventually decided that Henriette and Juliette should speak to the community at large and tell the Madames about their work on the streets of New Orleans.

It was a moment to be long remembered.

THIRTY-THREE

There were almost forty nuns, novices, and postulants gathered in the Chapter Room when Mother Praz introduced Henriette and Juliette.

"We have all come to know and to treasure our two visitors from the Children of the Holy Family in New Orleans. And, because they have conducted themselves in such an exemplary manner and have endeared themselves to all our community, I thought it might be instructive and edifying if they spoke to us about exactly what it is they do, what plans they have for the future."

Juliette got up first and could scarcely manage a whisper. Eyes cast down, very humbly, she said, "We are honored to be asked by you to speak in Chapter. We are overwhelmed. And all but speechless. But since I am always much more speechless than my dear friend and sister in Christ, Henriette Delille, I — I will ask her come to my rescue."

And Juliette sat down, covering her face with her hands. There was tittering among the nuns, who were quickly silenced when Mother Praz said, "Henriette, it appears that you are elected."

Henriette got to her feet, touched Juliette to comfort her, and then came forward to stand just a little to the right of Mother Praz's chair.

"Thank you, Mother Praz. I really don't know how to begin. We are only four in number, including our latest member, and we live in common in a house on Bayou Road. Our mission is to the slaves of the city, most particularly to the female slaves who have run away or who have been turned out or abandoned because of old age. Most of them are in the latter category.

"We do, of course, gather up and teach the slave children as best we can. Usually we can find only two or three at a time, and we teach them about Jesus, and redemption, and the love of God. Our purpose is to instruct these children until they are able to understand baptism, and then we baptize them or get them baptized by Father Rousselon, who is our dear friend, or by another priest."

Henriette paused, looking around uncertainly. "Go ahead, my child," Mother Praz said softly.

"Thank you, Mother." She took a deep breath. "Most of our time is spent with the older, usually dying, slave women. They do not know Jesus, and they usually receive word of him with great indifference, unless we are able — and have the time before they die — to tell them who he is, and what he means to their immortal souls. Many of these women we find on the streets, abandoned, left to die. They are clad in rags, they are plagued with disease, and often, especially if we find them around Congo Square, they have been beaten and robbed of everything, sometimes even of their clothing. They are lying naked or nearly naked in the mud when we find them, and they are sometimes quite mad — insane, I mean — and fight our attempts to rescue them. But, if we persevere, and we do, we are able to bring them back to our house. There we wash them, and cleanse their wounds, and dress them in whatever we have at hand. Some of them are truly grateful and sweet of nature and never stop thanking us. Some are not so grateful and spit and scratch and cry out in the night. But that is the devil at work, and we have learned that even the devil cannot stand up under loving kindness.

"Often these women are diseased in body. Awful sores and lacerations. Deep ulcers that really can't be excised without risking their very lives. Elephantiasis is the worst I have seen, especially when the disease is in the leg or the arms, and worms have invaded the body. It is necessary, I believe, to get these worms out. And that is not always easy. The creatures think they belong in the body, and they resist mightily. We used to pull them our with our fingers, by their little hard heads, but if you have a pair of medical forceps, it is much easier, and the worms are not able to bite you with their fierce little teeth."

At this point, a novice stood up, cried out, and fainted in place. Several nuns rushed to assist her. Henriette, who truly did not think the whole business was all that remarkable, looked dismayed and turned to Mother Praz. "I am sorry, Mother. Have I said enough?"

Mother Praz looked none to sprightly herself. "Yes, dear Henriette. I think we have heard quite enough for now. You may sit down."

Later, it appeared that several of the nuns had gotten physically ill during the night, and suffice it to say that Henriette was not asked again to speak at Chapter.

THIRTY-FOUR

Henriette wrote:

I have dreamed long and lovely dreams about coming to a place like this in my life and giving myself utterly over to God with the greatest pleasure, without the slightest reservation. Dreams, I say, without the slightest reproach for self-indulgence or guilt — simply a plunge into the heart of God without the requisite thought for the rest of the world, its horrors, its sorrows, or its agonies.

And now that I am here and have found that kind of incredible peace, realized those fantastic dreams, am I able to accept and surrender? Can I ease back into the bosom of my Lord, do my penances here and only here, and rest assured that I am doing the right thing, that I am following the fullest will of God?

I am afraid I cannot. I love it here with all my heart, could happily, delightedly stay here the rest of my days, in the scullery or wherever, and not give a thought to whatever lies beyond the walls.

But I have been beyond these walls, and I have seen and heard and smelled and, God help me, grown accustomed to the evil that is out there, and I know I must return to it, face it, and fight it in the name of my Lord Jesus Christ.

And I will, I shall, and I must prevail in his name. I wish and pray, as he did on the Mount of Olives, that this chalice might pass from me, but it will not, and I must rise up, go forth, and embrace it again with all my heart because... because that is God's will for me, and I will die tearing at that outer evil with all my strength, all my resolve, and all of my love.

But, dear God, how I would love to stay here, in the center of your Sacred Heart, in the sweetness and joy of these cloistered sisters, their walls, and their holiness. But I know I must go out amongst those others, back into the belly of the beast, and I shudder to think of it. Give me the will and the courage to go face it and fight it again, dear God, because the time is coming, and I grow weak and faint, and I dread the day I must pass out through these beloved gates.

Help me, Lord, to return to my cross and embrace it. Help me to carry it, as is my destiny in your divine plan, all the way up to the gates of heaven, where you will take it from me and say well done. For I shrink in the presence of your grace, I quake in the fear that I might fail thee, and I make the silent fist in the night and raise it to the devil, and I say to him "You will not bring me down, you will not snatch away my cross, you, wretched demon, will not seduce me from my

*true course, which is to live and die in the arms of my slaves,
in the awful stench of my own proper salvation."*

*Stand with me, dearest Jesus. Stand with me against the
beast, and prevent him from turning me in any least way
from doing your holy will. For I am not many things I
should be, I am not brave, but — heart, soul, and bowels —
I am thine.*

Amen.

THIRTY-FIVE

In late September of 1852, when their days at St. Michael's were
winding down, Henriette and Juliette spent at least an hour a day
in the convent library reading the lives of the saints and the rules
of those who had founded orders. The Rules of St. Augustine,
St. Benedict, St. Francis, and what they could find of the Desert
Fathers were read and notes were taken. When they were done —
two days before their departure — they decided upon the Rule of
St. Augustine, and Henriette, while thanking Mother Praz for
letting them use the rare books in the library, told her that they
had determined that the Rule of the bishop of Hippo was the
choice, whereupon Mother Praz presented Henriette and Juliette
with a copy of Augustine's Rule in French and Latin.

They wrapped it in butcher paper, put a ribbon around it, and
put it in Henriette's suitcase as the polestar by which she could
found their order.

Henriette received another book as a gift. Madame Susan
Blodgett, the precentrix in charge of the choir, gave Henriette
her autograph book: a beautifully bound volume containing hand-
written quotations, poems, drawings, spiritual sentiments, and, of
course, autographs signed by friends and some of the nuns. They
dated from Madame Blodgett's profession of vows through her

arrival at St. Charles, Missouri — the first American foundation of the Madames — through all her happy years at St. Michael's. The book was a tremendous gift, in view of what it had to mean to Madame Blodgett, and it was received by Henriette with great hesitation.

"No," Madame Blodgett said, "I haven't long to live, and this book will live on with you. Keep it in memory of me and the Madames of the Sacred Heart."

It was also wrapped in butcher paper, bound with a ribbon, and put in Henriette's suitcase as an earnest of her determination to live her life in God, as Madame Susan Blodgett had done.

The night before they left the convent, Henriette and Juliette went to the empty chapel, prostrated themselves on the stone floor in front of the high altar, and — arms out cruciform — dedicated themselves to the Sacred Heart of Jesus.

Henriette spoke in a firm voice. "My dearest Jesus, son of God, we pledge ourselves, our lives, our humble souls and bodies, to the service of your Sacred Heart. We are not worthy to speak to you in our own wretched words, and so we will speak in the words of beloved St. Gertrude. 'Hail, O Sacred Heart of Jesus, living and quickening Source of Eternal Life, infinite Treasury of the Divinity, burning Furnace of divine Love: thou art my Refuge and my Sanctuary. O my amiable Savior! Consume my heart with that burning fire with which thine is ever inflamed: pour down on my soul those graces which flow from thy love, and let my heart be so united with thine that our wills may be one, and my will in all things conformed to thine. May thy will be the standard and rule equally of my desires and of my actions. Amen.'"

They lay in place for more than two hours, got to their feet, embraced one another, and went off to sleep their last night in a convent not their own.

THIRTY-SIX

On November 21, 1852, Henriette Delille made her informal profession of vows. Standing before Archbishop Blanc and Father Rousselon in the Church of St. Augustine, this black woman raised her voice and loudly and joyously proclaimed her holy intention to be a bride of Christ and his church for the rest of her natural life.

Henriette had prepared herself to be firmly present for the event. She sang out almost fiercely, her voice like a trumpet announcing a new day: "I, Henriette Delille, in the name of our Lord Jesus Christ and his Holy Family, do hereby consecrate myself to God the Almighty, and I solemnly vow for the rest of my days to live in poverty, chastity, and obedience!"

And she stood there, tears starting in her eyes, looking toward the crucifix atop the altar, and murmured to herself, "Forever dear Jesus. No cross, no crown."

PART SIX

1853–1854

❧ ETIENNE ❧

THIRTY-SEVEN

Friday

New Orleans has the reputation of being the most unhealthy city in the world, and now, by God or despite him, it is beginning again! Since somewhere in the middle of May, when the first case of yellow fever was reported, I have braced myself, knowing what was coming, but praying hourly to God that it would not. And now, it seems, it is upon us in full fury, and there is no point in attempting to deny it. The forces of commerce have, of course, all arrayed themselves in complete denial. Commerce is king, they say, and anyone who would foul the skids of commerce by reporting a case of yellow fever should die the same death as he who has cried, "The king is dead!" And anyone who says this is not true simply does not know New Orleans. Officials have been quoted in the newspapers as saying that the early cases of the fever are merely "a slight sickness among visiting sailors and poor laborers who eat bad food." Madness! We know it is the onslaught of yellow fever, and anyone who says it is not is a self-serving, self-delusional fool!

Years ago, when I was recently arrived here, I was a typical civic dupe. I tried to pretend that what I was seeing and smelling was nothing more than the full flavor of a great burgeoning city, which, to be sure, has certain problems, but which will address and overcome all of these "blemishes" as soon as its "booming vitality" has slowed enough to allow it to take notice of the "few bruises and cuts" that have accrued along the way.

What infernal insanity! The full flavor of the city is an intolerable stench! And the blemishes are mortal, pus-filled cuts that stink to high heaven!

145

I fulminate, I know, but with very good reason. I remember, sometime back, reading the well-thumbed tract given me by my mysterious friend with the stickpin. At the time, I thought that he overstated everything, and his text could not possibly stand the test of pure reason. But I've just reread him, and, by my sober God, he had got it all almost exactly right! Listen to him on the subject of the most serious of civic blights, the graveyard system.

> The bodies of the dead are deposited in vaults or tombs, as they are called; yet all above ground, as it is impossible to dig a grave without the consequence of meeting water within a few inches of the surface of the ground. There is, however, a ridge of land about three miles from the city which is occupied as a burial ground, where the poor and the slaves are put in holes about two feet deep, and this is called the "Potter's Field." The old French depository for the dead lies in the rear of the center of the city, on the skirt of the swamp, yet it is surrounded by dwellings and may be considered as a part of the city. And a more gloomy, deathly, and pestiferous place cannot be found within the range of the civilized globe. And why such arrangements for disposing of the dead should be permitted is a matter of great astonishment to anyone who can reason from cause to effect. For there immediately within the heart and center of that city, enclosed in brick walls, lay thousands and tens of thousands of bodies in every possible state of decomposition that can be presented. And the odor from these vaults in hot weather is perceptible a great distance, and nearby is almost suffocating. And such is the stench within the enclosures that it brings on the most deathly and horrid sickness. And yet this is in New Orleans, and there it lies, and I know of no more proper place for such an arrangement, so "divil take the hindmost" as that is the rule by which all are governed....
>
> These grounds are about a mile in length and fifty or sixty rods wide. They are divided into three parts, all of which are enclosed in a solid wall of brick masonry about ten feet wide and nine feet high. In these long ranges of walls are holes resembling an oven, just large enough to slide in one coffin. When the coffin is put in, the opening is filled up with brick laid in mortar, and a small marble slab is also put in, cut on purpose to the shape of the opening, on which is the name and age of the deceased....

From the bottom of the wall close to the ground is the first opening or vault, and upwards one directly over the other are four more, and thus in the whole surface of the side and cross walls, as thick as can be allowed, are these "holes in the wall" as they are jokingly spoken of, making *graves* for thousands and tens of thousands who are being constantly swept into them by the bosom of destruction, made up from the malaria, the effluvia, from the swamps and city. And to render the *dose* complete, the exaltation from this great charnel house, this mass of corruption and death, is mingling with the sirocco that is pouring in upon them from every point, and is drunk down by the living mass who tread these streets as greedily as though it were the vital principle of their existence!

In my time, New Orleans has seen epidemics of yellow fever, cholera, and typhus, and in every event I have heard citizens and politicians saying that it was simply a minor case of swamp fever, nothing to be concerned about. This even in the face of the reputation of New Orleans, nationwide, as an unhealthy city, a place where even young men die. Malaria is considered a minor ailment even when one dies of it, and one hears all manner of attributions to the deceased's diet, his or her drinking habits, or Lord only knows what-all. Not once, *never*, have I heard anyone attribute the death, or several hundreds of deaths, to what I now consider the proper source — the lack of civic sanitation, starting with the incredible sprawl of the graveyards.

Well, it is bedtime, and I must wind down. Just one more note: it is now the twenty-second of June, weeks after the first cases of yellow fever were reported, and I read in the newspaper, the *Crescent,* the following: "But, of course, yellow fever has become an obsolete idea in New Orleans."

Dear God! We have more than a thousand dead since May, and every one of them dead of yellow fever, and yet they say that yellow fever is an obsolete idea! Are they all out of their minds? Do they think that God endures fools happily and forever? Do they think that we do not have an absolute obligation to our sick? That we can ignore...never mind. What is bothering me most at this moment is the thought of my dear Henriette going out bravely amongst them, risking infection and untimely death, without the slightest thought for her own safety. God, dear God, be with her and protect her, for she will do no other than her sacred honor compels her to do.

❧ HENRIETTE ❧

THIRTY-EIGHT

By the second week of July, more than two thousand people had died of it and even the newspapers were "bound to admit" that the city was in the throes of a yellow fever epidemic. The run on the burial vaults was clamorous. Hearse drivers battled for advantage in the funeral corteges, which stretched for miles along the roads to the cemeteries. "Trenches were dug," according to one account, "and many buried in a common grave covered with quick lime. The city appropriated wagons to call daily at homes to pick up corpses; these were known as 'Corporation Wagons.' The city also furnished rough box coffins painted with lampblack, known as 'Corporation Coffins.' New Orleans's streets were deserted, stores were closed; people remaining in the city huddled in their homes, making pitiful attempts to fight off the disease. It was a city of the dead."

Henriette and the women were swamped. They got the worst cases and almost none survived. Charles was busy morning to night hauling corpses off to Potter's Field, and even there the competition for gravesites was fierce. Charlie took to carrying an old battered trumpet and a huge butcher's cleaver. Waving the one and blowing on the other, he would find places to bury his wagonloads of dead.

Father Rousselon came by every morning to anoint the sick and the dying and then go on to Charity Hospital, which was packed beyond capacity. He'd spend all day anointing and hearing confessions and then come home to find lines standing in front of the old convent. He would go to bed around midnight and get up the next morning at dawn to find new lines already forming.

Henriette made a determination early on that, because of her lack of medical facilities, and because the functioning orphanages were already overrun, that she would concentrate on the children of the newly dead parents. She and the others would follow the Corporation Wagons around, and where the corpses of the father and mother had been collected, they would in turn collect the little children and bring them home to the house. Almost immediately, the house was wall-to-wall with children, a few of them sick, but most of them healthy, hungry, and frightened. The nuns begged for food to feed them; and food was forthcoming because, suddenly, there was a lack of demand for it. A city of the dead indeed.

During the week of August 7, 1853, 909 persons died of the fever. The following week was worse: 1288 died, more than 180 a day. Before it was over, in early October, the number of deaths from all causes in the city came to more than eleven thousand. The death toll, when finally reckoned, made the 1853 epidemic in New Orleans second only to the Black Plague in London in 1665. The cry from the Corporation Wagons — "Bring out your dead!" — raised the echoes of two hundred years before and left behind a city devastated, a population decimated, and a congregation of the faithful calling out to God for mercy and for forgiveness of the city's uncountable sins.

New Orleans was on its knees, and it stayed there for some several months — which, for New Orleans, was remarkable.

THIRTY-NINE

Father Jacques Pinchot, looking like he'd just been dragged a mile behind a freight wagon, came staggering into the Bayou Road house, collapsed on the nearest bench, and loudly announced: "No more! No more! They have just gone too far!"

Maria Pellerin, who was alone in the house with the five current patients — the others, including Magdaleine, being off helping the nuns at Mercy Hospital — came out into the front room, looked with some alarm at Father Pinchot, and said, "Why, dear Father, what has happened?"

"They knocked me down!" he said. "They pushed me out into the street and knocked me down in the slime!"

"Who did this?"

"The bastards! The rabble! The barbarians! They have pillaged me and my apartments! They have taken it all! The canned foie gras! The pickled pigs' hearts! The precious wines! My God, the wines! I saw one despicable wretch, who could pass for a vandal straight out of the Serbonian bogs, drinking — no, *guzzling* — a bottle of my private reserve Chateau Latour as if he were drinking *vin de pays* from a pisspot!"

"Father," Maria said, "you forget yourself."

"I forget nothing! They shall be made to make restoration! Every can of pâté, every can of caviar! I shall appeal to the diocese! I shall appeal to Rome! This sort of unmitigated outrage, the invasion of sacerdotal integrity, shall not be allowed to go unpunished! And I will have reparation, down to the last can and the last bottle!"

Maria looked at him with wonderment, and not a little disgust. "Father, there are people dying all over the city. From hunger, and from something pure to drink. You would begrudge them — ?"

"I *would* begrudge them!" he shouted, interrupting. "My quarters are a shambles! My rugs are fouled, my walls bespitted, my chair reduced to kindling, and my reds and ports and sherries — not to mention my sweet whites — are all despoiled! Carried off in the hands of ignoramuses who would not know a fine nose from a hog's snout!" He stared bug-eyed at Maria. "Where is Henriette Delille? She knows these swine! She wallows in them! Where might she be found, for they have started carrying off my books! Only she can bring a stop to it!" He fell back against the wall, arms out. The bench tilted forward and dumped him on his spine on the floor. He lay there, feet cocked on the side of the bench, and shouted, "Oh, Lord, why has thou forsaken me?" Then he appeared, quite abruptly, to pass out, his only movement the spittle bubbling out of his mouth and covering his lips and pointed chin.

Maria stood staring at him. What could she properly do? Men were not allowed in the building as patients. Not even priests. Yet here he was. She could not very well drag him out into the street. She shrugged, went to the linen closet, found a reasonably clean half-sheet, covered him with it, knelt down and said an *Ave,* and then began to cry. It was all too much. Even the clergy were being driven down. Father Pinchot wasn't much as a priest, and perhaps even less a man, but he was what they had, and lucky at that. But, dear God, where was it to end? And she found herself saying aloud, "Wherever it ends, dear Lord, I hope it is soon. I am near tether's end."

Then a woman in the back cried out loudly. Maria got to her feet slowly, blessed herself, and had just turned from the front door when it opened and in walked Henriette.

Henriette and Charles took Father Pinchot — still comatose — in Charles's wagon down to the Great Convent. Father Rousselon was summoned. He took one look at Pinchot and said, "The man is ossified. Put him in the cellarer's room."

When this was done, Father Rousselon invited Henriette up to his office, poured himself a small glass of swamp whiskey — all that was available — and spoke quietly to Henriette.

"How are things at Mercy?"

"We are doing well," Henriette said. "The number of deathly ill are waning. But, of course, they would have to. There cannot be many more left to die."

"No," Father Rousselon said. "I believe it is ending. I believe it is winding down. Thanks be to God. And you, dear Henriette, you too are winding down. You look thin and bone tired. Can you continue?"

"Of course, Father. But, if I may say so, you look worse than I have ever seen you. Are you eating?"

"Well," he smiled and shrugged. "I daresay I'm doing better than you are. Won't you have a sip of this ... this swamp water?"

"No, Father."

"It does lift one. For a brief time."

"Yes, I'm sure."

"No shadow of turning. Is that it?"

"No yielding to the shadow, Father. But, please, I do not judge you."

"Of course you don't." He sighed heavily. "Dear Henriette, if we survive this, promise me one thing?"

"Why yes, Father."

"Promise that you will accompany me — with suitable chaperon, of course — to a sumptuous, seven-course meal at the St. Charles Hotel? With wine and viands and all the trimmings?"

Henriette hesitated and then smiled. "I should be honored, Father. If I may bring the sisters."

"Bring whomever you like, dear friend. And we shall celebrate the risen city, the risen Christ, and the risen Jerusalem. In the name of the Father, the Son, and the Holy Ghost." He raised his glass, smiled gently, and sipped. "If God spares us, it is the least we could do."

Henriette smiled, got to her feet, bowed, and took her leave. As she cleared the door and turned to the stairs, she felt something like the stirrings of love for this man, Etienne. Something spiritual, to be sure, but something particular, personal, penetrating. She took hold of the balustrade, held herself for a moment, felt herself shudder, and then went quickly down the stairs, telling herself that she was acting like a novice.

Less than a week later, the fever began to fall away. The citizens of New Orleans — those who had survived — began to come out on the streets again, to walk in the sun, to believe that God had spared them. And they began to sweep the streets, put flowers on the graves, and tentatively to toot their horns, bang their drums, and return to the churches to give thanks that it hadn't been worse than it dreadfully had been.

PART SEVEN

1854–1857

❧ HENRIETTE ❧

FORTY

Henriette was scrubbing floors. Josephine, the tallest of the three, was scrubbing walls.

"They lost five sisters in the epidemic," Josephine said.

"Who?" said Juliette.

"The Sisters of Charity."

"Dear God," said Juliette.

"It's no wonder," said Henriette. "They are the bravest. They work and live right in amongst the patients."

"They are no braver than you are," Juliette said.

"If you speak of me, then you speak of all of us," Henriette said.

"But you are the bravest," said Josephine.

"Now, sister," Henriette said.

"It is as it is," said Juliette, interrupting.

"Where is Magdaleine?" Josephine said. "She still at her folks?"

"No," Henriette said. "At least I don't think so. She stopped by this morning, just after Mass, and said she would go out on the streets and beg."

There was a silence. "She's a good girl," Juliette said. "But she's too young and pretty to be begging."

There was another silence. Then Henriette said, "She will be our first novice, if all goes well."

There was a knock at the door. After a moment, as the women looked around at one another, the door was pulled open. There stood a short, broad-shouldered woman with eyes that snapped almost as sharply as her voice. She looked around, stepped forward into the house, and said, "I am Susanne Navarre. I am a seamstress from Boston, and I have come to join the Sisters of the Holy Family."

The women looked at Susanne Navarre for a moment and then looked around at one another. Then Juliette said, "Well, praise the Lord. Now maybe we got somebody to sew us up some habits."

"You are the Sisters of the Holy Family?" Susanne said, somewhat dubiously.

"Well, if we aren't," Juliette said, "we sure got a lot of folk fooled."

"They call you the servants of slaves?"

"Well, they call us a lot of things," Juliette said. "But that strikes very close to home. Come right in, Miss Boston."

FORTY-ONE

Because of their experience with children during the epidemic, the three foundresses decided that they would concentrate their energies on educating young women of color. Juliette's remark to the three orphan girls about having to sleep with dead slaves had made its point. They had been neglecting the living and the young in their zeal to baptize the dying. A better balance had to be struck. They decided to move one bed into the pantry (which seldom had any food on its shelves anyway) and turn the rest of the downstairs into classrooms and a small office. The elderly and dying would, most of them, be taken to the home for the elderly on St. Bernard Street or to Charity Hospital. The single-bed infirmary would be for extreme cases that could not be transported.

Juliette managed to talk the Jesuits on Baronne Street out of two bags of lime, and that took care of the whitewashing of the entire downstairs and the stairwell. Brother Tobias and Charles wrestled twelve desks out of the dark recesses of the Great Convent, and Father Rousselon gave some books, including a couple of dozen French-language catechisms. Susanne Navarre designed a prototype of the uniform the students would wear and sewed it together out of scraps of bed sheets and some toweling. The nickname "queen of the needle" was immediately bestowed upon her. Word was gotten out by means of small announcements posted on the notice boards of all the Quarter churches. Because there were still laws against the education of slaves, Henriette worded the announcements carefully. Free young ladies of color were openly invited to apply. Added to that was, "Any persons with the zeal for knowledge will be considered." It didn't work. Slaves were too frightened to seek an education, although some did show up in the evening for religious instruction.

Henriette was pleased nonetheless. Her little order was finally on a definable course, one that would win approval from church authorities when the time came to strike for formal recognition as an order of Catholic women.

On opening day, when the sixteen students were expected, all paying at least eighty cents a month (or whatever they could afford), Henriette knelt at the back of St. Augustine's Church and prayed: *"Bon Dieu Seigneur, you know my heart. You know what I have tried to do. I ask you to bless this latest effort. Through it our little congregation seeks to reach out to our lovely girls of color and teach them to honor your holy name and to conduct themselves in this world as obedient and cultivated daughters of your Holy Church. And to go on from there to take a place in this world that will elevate them to human respect, and give them the will and the grace to lead the black race out of the degradation of slavery, until they can assume the dignity you have intended for them since the foundation of the world as your people. Your holy people. Amen."*

❧ ETIENNE ❦

FORTY-TWO

Sunday

Well, it is late October and, thanks be to God, the horror is almost over. With the cooler weather, the "Knight of the Yellow Plume" has begun his retreat. What he leaves behind is almost beyond comprehension. Thousands dead, hundreds of orphans, whole families destroyed, and a city in deep mourning. Walking up to St. Augustine's this morning, I heard no night music, just a lone horn from somewhere near the blacksmith shop, and what he was playing was the *Dies Irae* of the Mass for the dead.

How anyone survived, I have no idea. There were days when I must have given extreme unction to fifty persons, heard any number of confessions and distributed Communions, sometimes to persons whom I knew had the fever, many times to persons who died of it. It was necessary to come close to the victims, touch them, and put my ear to their mouths to hear their sins. I did not disregard my own safety happily, but, rather, sacramentally. I merely did what had to be done and, by the grace of God, I escaped alive to tell of it.

The priests who did lose their lives I will record here as in a sacred necrology. Father J. E. Blin, newly assigned to St. Augustine's, a fine young man whom I liked; Father G. V. Gauthreaux of St. Mary's of the Archbishopric, our house chaplain; Father Anthony Parret, S.J., of Baton Rouge; Father M. Legendre of St. John the Baptist; Father Salmon of the Congregation of the Holy Cross; Father Plantazo; and Father Adams. Seven fine men, seven priests! Dear God, we could scarcely spare one of them, let alone seven. I have been bombarding France with letters to find replacements for them. So far, no responses. One can scarcely blame them for hesitating to

160

come to this civic charnel house. But I pray God some are moved to volunteer.

I shall name the nuns who died as well, brave souls who lived with the dying, fed and washed and stroked them until they died. All Sisters of Charity, they were: Sister Peregrina Hower; Sister Mary Maurice Whelan; Sister Octavia McFadden; Sister Lina Friffin; and Sister Mary Alfred Conway. I knew every one of them and buried four. Lovely, fresh-faced, utterly holy Irish girls who went cheerfully — no doubt of it — to meet their God. God rest them all. *Requiem aeternam dona eis, Domine, et lux perpetua luceat eis. Requiescant in pace. Amen.* And, merciful Lord, include those nuns whose names I do not have, two in Natchez and two in Mobile, who died on the crosses of their devotion to Christ.

Of my Henriette, my Josephine, and my Juliette of the Holy Family, all I can say is, thank you, dear God, for your tender mercies. They had no right to survive, because they were, every one, to my certain knowledge, walking the street day and night, bringing in the dead and the dying. And bringing in the children, the dead and dying, fearlessly, tirelessly, without the least thought to their own well-being. There were times when I thought they must be immune, so fierce and flagrant were their ministrations. Once I saw them bring a father, a mother, and an infant child to the side door at St. Augustine's when I was working there. By the time they laid them down, all three were dead. The three nuns knelt while I gave extreme unction and then began to cry and to *kiss* the faces of the victims. I know for a fact that they often went for a day and a night without sleep, pushed on until they literally fell over in faint. They were the bravest three people I have ever seen, or hope to see, and that God has his hand upon them is an absolute certainty as far as I am concerned.

And after all that? Why maybe their resiliency is the biggest miracle. The last I saw of them at 72 Bayou Road, they were busily whitewashing the inside of the house with exigent plans for starting a school for free young ladies of color! Where do we get such people! Where does God find them?

I must find some way to feed them. All three are skinny as birch trees, and there is, as far as I could see, no food in the house. Brother Tobias and I are conspiring to rob the pantry of the Great Convent to give them provisions, but we must find some more practical way to feed them until, at least, they begin to get money from tuitions. If they get any money, poor dears! What I heard was that they were thinking of asking for eighty cents per student per month!

Last week I was working late at the church, and Juliette suggested that I have dinner with them. I accepted, thinking they must have had some sort of a windfall. But when we got to the house, Henriette and Josephine — when Juliette said she'd invited me to dinner — looked at one another and turned away in confusion. It turned out that someone had promised them a bag of flour and some beans, but they had not been forthcoming. Dinner, as God is my witness, was to be sugared water! I couldn't believe it! I finally prevailed upon them to come down with me to the Great Convent and see what we might put together. Antoine was off to Lafayette, so Brother Tobias had a free hand. And, good Gascon that he is, he put together a lamb stew with rosemary that was fit for — well, it was fit for the three holiest people I know. They were persuaded to take the leftovers — a few loaves of bread and a half-bottle of wine — home with them to feed the new recruits Magdaleine and Susanne Navarre, who had been out begging when we left. I could have wept to see how sparingly they ate, and how they kept looking around as if to see if there might be someone — anyone — more hungry than they. I tell you, Death may still be walking the streets of New Orleans, but there are saints walking right beside him, and, epidemic to the contrary, my money is on the saints.

❧ HENRIETTE ❧

FORTY-THREE

"I will go out looking this afternoon," Henriette said. "You may come along if you like."

School was out. The twelve students had gone home for the day. Josephine and Magdaleine were out begging. Juliette was collecting altar cloths and linen vestments for laundering. And Henriette and Susanne Navarre were busily sewing new uniforms for the students, all of whom had paid their tuition for the month (which had finally been fixed at ninety cents). Susanne had taken the money and bought materials enough for the uniforms (each student would pay two dollars), and the school seemed successfully launched.

"Well, I don't think you'll find any truants. The poor things all died of the fever."

"Yes, but I must look," Henriette said. "The poor things have no one else. Especially now."

"Well, I believe I'll let you go alone," Susanne said. "I'll do my sewing, and if one of them shows up, I'll be here."

"Very well," Henriette said. "But the slaves almost never come by themselves. Even if they are able, they would not presume — which is a shame."

"And I'll put sheets on the pantry bed," Susanne said. "Just in case."

"Thank you, Susanne. You have been a godsend."

"God sends the work. I do it."

Henriette nodded, glancing over at what Susanne was doing at the corner of a collar. "Oh," she said, "now I see."

"You're doing very well," Susanne said, "for someone who hasn't done much sewing."

"I'll learn." A couple of moments passed in silence. "You never told me how you found us, Susanne. After all, we aren't that well known."

"Better than you might think." Susanne stilled her needle for an instant and then nodded. "Yes. It was that Redemptorist priest. He was the first."

"Who was he?"

"Oh, he was up from Baltimore. Came to preach a mission at our church in Dorchester." She smiled and nodded. "A handsome man with white hair. A friend, he said, of your archbishop."

"Archbishop Blanc?"

Susanne frowned. "Yes. And he said that there was a community of lay women — free colored women — in New Orleans, and that they were looking for help. I listened." Susanne smacked her lips and darted her eyes. "And here I am."

"Well, we are delighted to have you here," Henriette said.

"Of course, I didn't know there were only three or four of you. But that is of no account. I mean to join you."

"You already have."

"And I mean to sew us our habits, when they say we can."

"That will be wonderful. Father Rousselon says that Archbishop Blanc thinks we might expect recognition from Rome in two or three years. Of course, they take their time."

"They certainly do. If women were running things it wouldn't take three days. But we haven't had a woman pope in years."

"Oh, Susanne, I don't think there was ever a woman pope."

"Is that right?"

"As far as I know."

"Well," Susanne snorted, "no wonder everything takes so long."

And after a moment they both began to laugh softly.

FORTY-FOUR

As the year wore on toward Christmas, the house on Bayou Road was transformed, often filled with the laughter of the students and their teachers (which now included Susanne, who was teaching sewing and knitting, and Magdaleine, who had proved to have a lovely singing voice and was teaching choir), and, quite often, the hearty laughter of the archbishop and of Father Rousselon, both of whom were devoted friends and sponsors.

And the joy upon the house had very much to do with a change, a certain change, in the mind and disposition of Henriette. She had entered into a phase of her spiritual life that had begun with her reading of St. Teresa of Avila's life (she borrowed, and borrowed again Father Rousselon's copy), and had now begun her reading of another of Father Rousselon's books: *The Dark Night of the Soul* by St. John of the Cross, who, in 1572, was confessor to the nuns at the Convent of the Incarnation at Avila, when Teresa was prioress of that convent.

St. John of the Cross's book seemed to consume her. She read it while sewing, while walking the streets, while the rest of the house was asleep. When she returned it to Father Rousselon he had asked her almost in jest if she had done any memorizing, as she had with St. Teresa of Avila's life. Whereupon Henriette had recited all eight of the Stanzas of the Soul.

1. On a dark night, Kindled in love with yearnings — oh, happy chance! —
   I went forth without being observed, My house being now at rest.

2. In darkness and secure, By the secret ladder, disguised — oh, happy chance! —
   In darkness and in concealment, My house being now at rest.

3. In the happy night, In secret, when none saw me,
   Nor I beheld aught, Without light or guide, save that which
   burned in my heart.

4. This light guided me. More surely than the light of noonday
   To the place where he (well I knew who!) was awaiting me —
   A place where none appeared.

5. Oh, night that guided me, Oh, night more lovely than the
   dawn,
   Oh, night that joined Beloved with lover, Lover transformed
   in the Beloved!

6. Upon my flowery breast, Kept wholly for himself alone,
   There he stayed sleeping, and I caressed him, And the
   fanning of the cedars made a breeze.

7. The breeze blew from the turret As I parted his locks;
   With his gentle hand he wounded my neck. And caused all
   my senses to be suspended.

8. I remained, lost in oblivion; My face I reclined on the
   Beloved.
   All ceased and I abandoned myself, Leaving my cares
   forgotten among the lilies.

She spoke softly, and ever more softly, her eyes modestly down, and when she had finished, she was perfectly still, and the silence in the room expanded.

At last, Father Rousselon, also speaking softly, said, "That was very beautiful."

"Yes," she said. "I'm sure you know it well."

"Not nearly as well as you do."

"Well," she said, "you will, when you give yourself time." Then she got suddenly to her feet, excused herself, and walked quickly from the room. After a moment, she looked back in. He hadn't moved. "Merry Christmas, Father," she said, and was gone.

❧ ETIENNE ❦

FORTY-FIVE

"We understand you have taken to drinking in public, Father." Archbishop Antoine was at his sternest, and his tone reflected it. He stared across his desk at Father Pinchot, who slumped in his chair, his eyes hooded, his aspect that of a caught felon, his clothing bespattered, rumpled, even his Roman collar with a ring of dirt around it.

Now he issued a sort of yelping, dismissive laugh. "Oh, no, no. I assure you. That is much exaggerated. I have stopped in a place for a glass of water from time to time...."

"Father, you have been seen to spend whole afternoons and evenings in places like the Ruby, the Orleans, and the Sazerac. There is even evidence that you have taken up absinthe."

Another wretched chuckle. "Absinthe! Oh, Bishop, I don't know who the source of these lies is, but I—"

"I am the source of these 'lies,' Father," I said. "And they are not, of course, lies."

"Oh, but Father, I must protest! I...I have been very circumspect about—"

"There are also certain irregularities concerning funds donated to the St. Augustine's building fund that were put into your care. Some monies have been missing for seven or eight years."

"The building fund? Monies? I know nothing of these things."

Antoine pushed forward a stack of bank drafts and cheques on the desk before him. "Look these over, Father. Every one of them bears your signature in endorsement, and not one penny has shown up on the ledgers. They amount to a sum of almost four thousand francs, or in dollars—"

167

Now Pinchot interrupted. "No, Bishop, this cannot be! You know I have my own income! These piddling funds would mean nothing to me!"

Antoine leaned forward, his brows knit. "Enough, Father Pinchot! Do you take us for fools? You have been disinherited! I have here a letter from the legal offices representing your parents' estates. They will no longer be responsible for your bills, the loans you have floated, or your letters of credit."

"No, no, Bishop. That is all a misunderstanding! I have the complete confidence of my family. They are entirely loyal." He paused, worked up a sort of scowling smile. "Except, of course, for my brother, Pierre. He has always hated me."

Antoine scowled at him, then sighed, and pushed back in his chair. "Father Pinchot, you are in a state of disintegration. I'm not sure how you got that way, but it appears you were well along when you came to us. Now, you will either pull yourself together — start by washing your person and your clothes, continue by attending properly to your priestly duties, and end free use of alcohol, tobacco, and all other excesses — or you will be on your way back to France before middle-March! And that is my episcopal promise!"

Father Pinchot stared at him, blinking, his eyes filling with tears. "Oh God, oh no, oh Jesus." Then, *"But* of course, your Grace!"

And by virtue of some last despairing energy, he managed to struggle to his feet and bestow a ghastly smile upon Antoine. "You are my lord and my ordinary and I give you my parole that you will never have occasion to remonstrate with me again, my lord." And he turned, took a purposeful stride toward the door, and fell full on his face.

I leaped up to assist him, but he scrambled up at once, managed to reach the door, and went out without a backward look.

I turned to find Antoine with his head in his hands. "Dear God in heaven. His parole, no less. The man is reprobate."

"I will see to him more closely, Antoine."

"Is he still treating Miss Delille shabbily?"

"Yes, I'm afraid so. He's even called her the instrument of the devil, sent, with her feigned saintliness, to bring him down."

"Dear Jesus. Perhaps we ought to have the man confined."

"Every Mass he says, every confession he hears is a blessing just now, Antoine."

"Or a sacrilege," Antoine said, heaving himself to his feet. "Well, my good Etienne, see to him as best you can. Of Christ's crosses there seems to be an endless supply."

And he went out, heavy at the shoulders, and, at that moment, I could have happily shipped Monsieur Jacques Pinchot back to Lyon in a case of caviar tins.

❧ HENRIETTE ❧

FORTY-SIX

Henriette wrote:

Father Pinchot continues to be a complete mystery. I have no idea what to make of him, and I avoid him whenever possible. I should not do this, in Christian charity, but he makes any personal contact an embarrassment. Father Rousselon remains pastor of St. Augustine's but is obviously so busy with the business of the diocese that he has had to leave most of the pastoral duties to Father Pinchot. I have not lately complained to Father Rousselon — what can he do? He is not omnipotent. So we endure. And the situation has become more and more agonizing and even, in some respects, ludicrous.

Father Pinchot has taken to wearing a rough, undyed woolen habit with a black belt to gather it at the middle and has grown a long, straggly beard which is dirty yellow, exactly the color of the habit. He now wears sandals and has toenails fully an inch long. He has neglected his teeth and lost several of his frontals. When he turns to bless us during the Mass he invariably smiles, and it is hideous. Sometimes, when he has the altar wine dripping down into his beard and he is saying his Mass in his sing-song, tip-toe manner, we are often reduced to subdued laughter, to epidemic giggles.

Of course, he mostly confines this behavior to the early morning, when he knows Father Rousselon is not likely to be around. But it often recurs during the day. In confession, for example, he is most abusively rude. He will shout, so that

170

all in the church can hear, "What did you do that vile thing for? Don't you know it dooms you to hellfire?" Then, even worse, he will whisper the word "harlot" or "voodoo" very clearly and intensely, and slam the slide shut, without giving a penance or absolution.

He has taken to leering at poor Maria so openly that the dear child is afraid to approach the communion rail. He will lick his tongue across his lips and, breaking from the Latin, will whisper, "Comely black whores do not go to heaven! You need my counsel!" Or, "Let us repent together!"

Often, when by chance I encounter him in the corridors or on the street, he will glare at me, his eyes blazing, and, when I am fully past him, will say very softly but intensely, "Black skin, black heart!" Or, "Hypocrite in a black suit!" Or even, "You don't fool me, nonvirgin!"

The worst of it was a few mornings ago at the conventual Mass. While glowering directly at me, he gave as his text a passage from a poet he identified as Spenser. As best I remember it, it went as follows:

> *Her nether parts the shame of all her kind,*
> *My chaster muse for shame doth blush to write*
> *For at her rump she growing had behind*
> *A fox's tail with dung all foully dight!*

I knew that he was in one of his worst fits, and I saw no point in staying in place. I indicated to Juliette to take the others from the chapel, and I followed them as he called after me, "Go, go, you dissembler! Your winding sheet is being wound!"

God tells us to reach out to our oppressors, to forgive the misguided, to love those who hate us. I shall persevere, and

I shall not complain again to Father Rousselon. But I am very much afraid that this man is quite mad, that he has taken complete leave of his senses, and that God himself must intervene to save him from complete howling insanity. If he is not already there. I have told our little community that we must endure, and we shall. We are doing very well, aside from Father Pinchot, and we will happily bear up under our burdens and keep the stricken Christ in the forefront of our holy vision.

    Amen.

❧ ETIENNE ❦

FORTY-SEVEN

Thursday

Two days ago, on September 18, Antoine was out in the parishes checking on yellow fever victims and fell through a hole in the wharf at Donaldsonville, breaking his leg. It was a compound fracture, infection was almost immediate, and he is in great pain. I can do nothing to help, and I'm afraid that what I am feeling is anger. We have had quite enough of pain lately.

The last twelve months have been a punishment, for what I am not sure. It began when the Know-Nothings — also known as the Nativists or the American Party — began their campaign against the immigration of Europeans into the United States, many of them entering through New Orleans. These latter were largely German and Irish, and though many of the Germans were Protestants, almost all of the Irish were Roman Catholics. So the outcry quickly became an anti-Catholic crusade with all the usual nonsense of papal domination of American politics, church interference in political decisions, Jesuitism, the baneful influence of bishops and clergy, allegiance to a foreign potentate, and all the rest of that particular madness. It was this sentiment, and indeed this party, that so long prevented Antoine from taking his proper place in St. Louis Cathedral. This was troublesome enough, but it all took a much more vicious turn last fall in Plaquemines Parish. I write it down now because only now have I sufficiently overcome my revulsion to treat of it, and of its effects.

Father Savelli was pastor of St. Thomas's Church at Pointe-a-la-Hache. He was a good and holy man, foreign-born, of course, and not an American citizen. Led by Know-Nothing agitators, his congregation began to plot against him. They decided to lure him out at night with a pretended sick call. Shortly after he left his house, he was ambushed by some twelve conspirators. They stabbed him thirty-six times. Then they dragged his body to the church, stripped his body of clothing, mutilated him, and threw his organs in the river. Then somebody found an old bathtub outside. They dragged it into the church, put the poor priest's body in it, and poured a keg of whiskey they had brought along for the celebration into the tub. And although the whiskey was mixed heavily with the priest's blood, they drank of it wildly, celebrating until dawn.

How such things happen I have no idea. We sent Father J. B. Langlois out there about six months ago, and he found a penitent and subdued congregation, as apparently shocked by the events as one would expect, and peace now reigns in Plaquemines Parish.

But, dear God, how *can* such things be? Where does such virulence come from? Is it simmering even now beneath the surface of our apparent calm, ready to erupt when the next agitator comes out of the woodwork? Is Christ's Kingdom so tenuous on American soil?

I'm afraid that it is, just as I am afraid that Antoine's accident was no accident. I have no proof, no evidence, but I do have my doubts. Two of the three men walking with him were "former" Know-Nothing sympathizers and could easily have led Antoine into a weak part of the decking. No one was within ten feet of him when he fell, and Antoine is such a trusting person that he would follow a demon into fire if he didn't have someone like me along to warn him. I wasn't there and I should have been. I blame myself, and I will not permit myself to rationalize it.

My dear Henriette's community is not exactly thriving, but, beside Susanne Navarre — who is an incredible seamstress — two other able women have joined the little community and have taken private vows to serve the church. These are Orphise François and Harriet Fazende. There is also Jeanne Marie Aliquot, a fairly wealthy woman from what I can gather, who has loaned money to Henriette and the order at various times. Although she has not joined them, she is beloved of the other women and entirely devoted to them.

It is very much on my mind to get this little community properly recognized by Rome, to get them established under a formal rule of religious life, with their own distinctive religious habit and with the full privileges of pronouncing the vows of poverty, chastity, and obedience. This is what Henriette so fervently wants, and this is what I am working fervently to get for her.

It is amazing how much she occupies my mind. Even more amazing is the conviction that it is her work and her holiness before God that is keeping the entire Archdiocese of New Orleans from going to hell in a flaming basket.

PART EIGHT

1860–1861

❧ HENRIETTE ☙

FORTY-EIGHT

By May of 1860 the community numbered six: Henriette, Juliette, Josephine, Susanne Navarre, and newcomers Orphise François and Harriet Fazende. Magdaleine Chaigneauy, beautiful voice and all, had for some time been finding the austere life simply too difficult to bear. She hated begging, and one day, after soloing in a Palestrina Mass at St. Patrick's, she was approached by a musical impresario and succumbed to his promises of the finest training for grand opera.

Jeanne Marie Aliquot was not a member of the community, but unofficially everyone called her "sister." Some of the clergy had from time to time suggested that Miss Aliquot might better direct her energies by joining an order of white nuns, but after spending a few months with the Visitation Sisters in Mobile, Alabama, she left, saying that she too much missed her beloved Holy Family and working with the slaves.

The community's work was overwhelming. The school was thriving, with twenty-one young girls enrolled. The after-school catechism classes continued for poor slave children. The hospice of the elderly on St. Bernard Street had become too small to accommodate those who truly needed help. Henriette was therefore hard at it trying to raise funds to build an annex on Hospital Street. She had long since begun visiting the homes of the sick — the homes *and* the hovels — and was also on call to visit sick slaves at the homes of their masters or in the slaveyards and Congo Square. She was often helped by the others, but Henriette was first on call, first to serve.

Visiting the sick involved, first, cleaning the house and scrubbing down the victim and the children and, second, preparing the victim to meet his or her God. Short prayers were taught and repeated: "Jesus, in your love I wish to live, Jesus in your love I wish to die." As always, the priest was sent for at the point of death for the last rites. After the victim passed, if the children could not be placed with relatives, the community had more children to care for. These orphans were so numerous that Henriette and her companions had to open a house on Dauphine Street, which sheltered the orphans and provided a free school for them and for abandoned slave children.

The priests at St. Augustine's and St. Mary's on Chartres, and later at the cathedral, had to get used to being led by one or another of the women — but mostly by Henriette — to the most incredibly wretched and out-of-the-way places in the city to administer the last rites to some dying person. "How in hell does she find them," they would say. "Does she have a 'moment of death' patrol?" Father Rousselon never asked. He knew.

And he also knew that her unflagging devotion to her slaves and the destitute was beginning to take its toll on Henriette's health. He knew she was not eating well, and he would go down to her after Mass from time to time and ask if she and one or two of the other women in the community would like to have dinner with him at the Great Convent. She would always thank him profusely, but regretfully refuse: there was simply too much to do that day, that evening, far into the night. Then how about seeing a doctor? An excellent man Etienne knew. No, no, Henriette would say. She was fine, and, full of smiles and waves, she would virtually run from him.

But Henriette knew he was right, and there were days when she could barely force herself out of bed at 4:30 a.m., could scarcely bend to find her shoes, could scarcely kneel at Mass. But she attacked those days, fiercely, telling the devil he would have to find himself another mark, as this one was too busy for him and

his damned wiles. And if she needed inspiration, she thought of
Archbishop Blanc.

Broken leg and all, intense pain to the contrary, Antoine
Blanc was not giving an inch. Despite the protestations of Father Rousselon and the rest of the clergy, he was continuing his
full schedule, including visiting the seminary and the priests and
nuns in the parishes near and far. He gritted his teeth and went
resolutely against the barb of his improperly healed leg.

Henriette prayed for the archbishop constantly and told herself
that if he had to put up with such pain, how could she not. She
whose pains were incidental, mere slivers of the cross.

❧ ETIENNE ❧

FORTY-NINE

Monday

Antoine collapsed and died this morning while working on correspondence in his office. Father Pinchot, who was sitting in the parlor awaiting an audience, heard a sharp cry from within. Pinchot rushed in and found the archbishop fallen across an office couch, unable to speak or move. I was summoned at once and just had time to administer the last rites before, with a great sigh, he died. He was looking at me intently when he breathed his last, but he did not manage to speak a word.

Dear God! I knew that leg would kill him. It had never healed and had developed a low infection and, lately, a certain odor. He said there was nothing doctors could do — although several tried — and he ceased seeing them when they began to talk about cutting it off. The pain was obviously intense, but he pressed on, saying that his work wasn't done and could not be neglected.

I mourn him, I venerate him, I weep in the night. I loved him as a brother, as a companion, as the center of my universe. I rose in the wee hours to go and sit by his corpse and to brush the flies away. And I prayed that God would rest his dear soul, that he would be waiting for me when I passed, and that God would give me the strength to carry on in a manner that would do honor to his memory. There will be another bishop, and I will serve him to the best of my ability. But there will be a great hollowness about it all without Antoine. And, as Henriette would say, there will be a long loneliness for me until Antoine and I are together again.

Antoine's body lay in state at St. Mary's adjoining the Great Convent on June 20 and 21. At 5:00 p.m. on the 21st, it was brought to the cathedral, which he had fought so long to restore to the archbishopric. At 8:00 a.m., June 22, I helped Bishop Elder of Natchez — the only bishop able to attend — to say a Solemn High Mass of Requiem. At 5:00 p.m., his body was interred in the floor of the cathedral sanctuary.

Somewhere between Mass and interment I was called upon to preach the eulogy. Grief had come over me so strongly and profoundly that I could barely be heard, which was probably just as well because the sermon was perfect drivel. I recited long lists of Antoine's accomplishments and statistics, but while my mouth was saying words, my soul was melting with sorrow. I said that since 1835, he added sixty-five priests to the archdiocesan roster (looking at Father Pinchot, I almost added "including one insufferable piss-ant"). I said that he had established a seminary, two colleges, nine academies and schools, four orphanages, one hospital, and one home for girls. I wound up by saying we had lost a bishop, God had gained a saint, and I had lost my best friend in life. And then I broke down and started to weep. I managed to whisper an amen and then proceeded to fall down the steps of the pulpit. I almost landed on Pinchot, which, had I accomplished it and done him bodily harm, would have written a fitting end to the obsequies.

I knelt in the night at the altar rail of St. Mary's and said my goodbye to Antoine.

"Antoine," I said aloud, hearing my own echo, "now you know. We talked from time to time about that awful doubt that sometimes comes over you at the moment of consecration, when you doubt that you are a worthy priest, that you have the power to command the presence of Jesus, even that the host could possibly become the Body and Blood of Christ. Well, dear Antoine, no more of that. Now you are in his presence; now you know. And I know that, because you are there, I will never doubt again. But I will miss you, Lord God, I will miss you! Your kindly eye, your laughter, your gentle way with me and with all you touched. I envy God your presence, and I am graceless in my refusal to let you go.

"But do go, Christian soul, out of this world, in the name of God the Father almighty who created you; in the name of Jesus Christ, Son of the living God, who suffered for you; in the name of the Holy Spirit, who was poured out upon you. Go, Antoine, and in the hour of my death, remember me, as I have remembered you."

So, God help me, I ended thinking of myself. So be it. I got to my feet as dawn lighted the windows and walked out of the church with my heart as heavy as a great stone.

❧ HENRIETTE ❦

FIFTY

The year between the bombardment of Fort Sumter on April 12, 1861, and the bombardment of New Orleans in April 1862 was the worst of times for Henriette and her sisters. The sound and the fury of the oncoming war filled the city. Everyone from pimps to politicians to priests filled the air with argument about right and wrong, secession and slavery, the holy South and the demon North. Husbands and fathers, sons and lovers lined up to don the gray uniform of the Confederacy, and hundreds of male slaves were left to defend the households of those who had gone off to fight to keep them in slavery.

When the Union troops occupied the city, they found that they were in hostile territory indeed. Young women would have nothing to do with the Union soldiers, and the older women made sure that the young women stayed in line. Women would cross the street when they saw a Union soldier or officer approaching, and some women cursed and taunted Union troops from their balconies and emptied slop buckets on their heads. In church, if Union troops were present, the women would pretend to be violently ill and depart, retching, until the Union blues were left in the pews by themselves.

It all got to the point where a certain Major General Butler issued a directive, General Order Number 28, dated May 15, 1862. It read:

> As the Officers and Soldiers of the United States have been subject to repeated insults from the women calling themselves ladies of New Orleans, in return for the most scrupulous noninterference and courtesy on our part, it is

185

ordered that hereafter when any Female shall, by word, gesture, or movement, insult or show contempt for any officer or soldier of the United States, she shall be regarded and held liable to be treated as a woman of the town plying her avocation.

By command of
Maj.-Gen. Butler George C. Strong
A. A. G. Chief of Stables.

This meant a soldier could complain of harassment by a woman and cause her to be arrested, held overnight in jail, brought before a magistrate, and required to pay a five-dollar fine or returned to prison.

The "Woman Order" raised an outcry heard coast to coast, in Europe, and in all the civilized capitals of the world. The General Order was published on front pages from New Orleans to San Francisco under headlines: "An Outrageous Insult to the Women of New Orleans!" And "Southern Men, Avenge Their Wrongs!"

Many women defied the order. A certain Mrs. Anne Larue pinned a secessionist flag to her bodice and caused a near riot. They convicted her and sent her to solitary confinement on Ship Island for an undefined period. A Mrs. Philip Philips stood on her balcony and laughed loudly at the funeral procession of a Union officer passing below. She was also sent to Ship Island.

By the end of June, the streets of New Orleans were unsafe for a decent woman to walk, no matter how carefully she minded her manners.

By the time she got to Congo Square, Jeanne Marie Aliquot was exhausted. She had walked from the Bayou Road house under a flat, white sun that baked the air into a brown meringue that tasted of dust and the bodies of the dead frying in their vaults. The girl's tent was fortunately on the near side of the Square, so she didn't have to go in among the mass of slaves, most of them squatting on their haunches, staring balefully at anything that moved. In the distance, through the heat waves, she thought she could see some people dancing langorously and could hear the thumping of drums and the sounds of several horns blowing out dissonant notes like mynah birds in a dismal swamp.

As she approached the oilcloth shelter, she saw one of the brothers of Essie, a student at the sisters school, out front, sitting on an upturned wooden bucket.

"Hello," she said. "My name is Jeanne Marie. Essie is a student at our school."

The boy nodded and blinked in the sun.

"I came to inquire about Essie. She hasn't been to class."

"Dunno," said the boy.

"Could I speak to your mother?"

The boy gestured toward the inside of the shelter.

Jeanne Marie stepped past the boy and put her head in at the tent-flap entrance. The front of the room was empty. Jeanne Marie called out softly, "Hello?"

And it was then that she saw movement behind a sheet hung as a screen across the back of the room.

She heard a woman's voice say sharply, "Who's that?"

Then a man's voice: "Never mind, never mind!"

Jeanne Marie pulled back as a the boy grabbed a pinch of her skirt and yanked at it.

"There. Red-haid. He done it." The boy pointed his finger.

Jeanne Marie turned to see a tall Union soldier with carrot-red hair standing by the guard-box just outside the Square.

"What did he do?" asked Jeanne Marie.

"He done Essie," the boy said.

"You hush your face!" A woman came out of the shelter, fastening her skirt. She cuffed the boy and sent him scurrying with a kick before turning on Jeanne Marie. "What you doin' here, causin' trouble?"

187

"Now wait, now wait here," said a huge black man coming out of the shelter. "This here's one of them sisters. You show some respect."

"Don't you tell me!" She wheeled on Jeanne Marie. "What you want here?"

"I work with the sisters of the Holy Family. Essie has been one of our catechists, and I am here to find out why she has not been to class these past two weeks."

"Told you," the man said.

"You hesh up, Purvis!" the woman said. "She don't look like no holy sister to me. More like white trash."

"They *kilt* her," the boy said, peering around the corner of the shelter.

"I toll you!" the woman said, starting for the boy, who ducked quickly out of sight.

"Sorry to be the one, Sister," Purvis said. "But them soldier boys took her out in the swamp and had their way with her."

"Shut up, Purvis!"

"And then they kilt her and buried her in the mud."

Jeanne Marie stood staring. "My dear God. You know this to be true?"

"He don't know nothin'!"

"Well," said Purvis. "I wasn't there. But one of them boys did a little braggin'."

"Are you Essie's mother?" Jeanne Marie said.

"I ain't none of your business!"

"She's the mother," Purvis said.

"Are you the father?"

"Oh no. He run off."

"Can you take me to the grave?"

"Ain't much grave left. Dogs got the body."

"Oh, my God," Jeanne Marie said. She could feel sweat running down her body underneath her heavy dress.

"I got this," Purvis said. He took a small blue handkerchief from his pocket and handed it to Jeanne Marie.

Jeanne Marie took the handkerchief. "Yes," she said. "I remember this . . . the yellow border."

"Only pretty thing she had," Purvis said.

"Did you report this?"

"Well, I would, but you cain't but *re*-port to the soldiers, and them's the ones did it," Purvis said.

"Well, I'm going to report it anyway. To a magistrate, and name the soldiers, if I can." She turned, pointed to the red-headed soldier. "You're sure he was one of them?"

"He was the leader," Purvis said.

"Do you know his name?"

"Never mind his name!" the woman said. "You go messin' with him, you wish you hadn't of!"

"Well, I'm going to mess with him," Jeanne Marie said.

"Then I ain't her mother!" the woman said, shouting. Jeanne Marie looked slowly around at her. "Essie was your daughter, a beautiful girl. Your own flesh and blood. Given to you by God as the purest of gifts. The holiest of sacred trusts. And you — you'd deny your motherhood?"

"I surely would!"

"Shame on you!" Jeanne Marie said. "Shame and mortification!"

"You'd best watch your tongue, woman!"

"You'd best look to your soul!" Jeanne Marie said sharply.

The woman started to speak, her lips quivering. Then she burst into tears. "She done put a curse on me!"

Purvis stepped forward and put an arm around the woman. "She don't mean nothin'," he said. "We's just tryin' to stay out of trouble."

"But you can't allow rape and murder to go unpunished."

Purvis shook his head. " 'Fraid we can, Sister. 'Fraid we got to."

"Well, *I* don't got to," Jeanne Marie said. And she turned on her heel and started to stride toward the guardhouse.

The red-headed soldier looked at Jeanne Marie out of close-set, mean little eyes. "What did you say?"

"I said that you are responsible for the rape and murder of Essie Hitchins. And I am directing you to come with me to the magistrate."

"Lady, I don't know what you're talking about, but you'd best watch your mouth, or *I'll* take *you* to the magistrate."

"On what charge?"

"Well, for one thing, you got them gray flags on your dress."

"They are not flags. They are patches."

"I guess I'll be the judge of that."

"Are you going to come with me?"

"No, I believe you're going to come with me."

"I'll be the judge of *that*," Jeanne Marie said.

"Hey, Cyrus!" the soldier said, shouting at the guardhouse. "Got me a arrest here! Going to take this here crazy woman down to the judge!"

Cyrus came out of the guardhouse and took a long, appreciative look at Jeanne Marie. "Tough duty, Wicklow. You be sure to keep your pants on."

"Come on, then," Wicklow said to Jeanne Marie. "You march two steps ahead of me."

"I will walk where I please."

Wicklow slipped his rifle from its shoulder sling and pointed it at Jeanne Marie. "Walk, woman, or by God I'll drop you where you stand."

Jeanne Marie rose as ordered and addressed the magistrate, a kindly looking Southern man with a well-trimmed white beard. "Your honor. I am here not to answer charges, but to press them. Against Corporal Wicklow. But first, to answer, my dress as you can see, is patched. It is patched because I choose to live in poverty, and I would not spend money on a new dress if I had it. I would give the money to the poor. So when my dress becomes worn, I, like my sisters in religion, patch my dress with whatever comes to hand. Sometimes gray cloth is what is available, and that is what I use. The gray in my dress is no flag, except perhaps the flag of poverty."

The magistrate looked down on her benignly. "My dear lady, are you not one of those sisters? The Holy Family, I believe?"

"I am not a sister, your honor, but I work with them."

"Corporal Wicklow, you bring a woman into court because she's got a few gray patches on her dress? I also see red, white, and blue patches, the colors of your flag. Are you color-blind, or are you just an idiot?"

"Just trying to do my duty."

"Charge dismissed," said the magistrate. "Now, dear lady, about this rape and murder charge?"

Jeanne Marie gathered herself and presented the circumstances as well as she could, ending with: "And in view of all this, I think Corporal Wicklow ought to be held to answer."

"It's all lies, Judge! She made it all up!"

"Sit down, Corporal. And be quiet, or I'll have you removed." Then to Jeanne Marie, "My dear, in order for your allegations to have any chance of success, you must get the primary accusers before this court. The mother, the son, this man Purvis. Do you think you can do that?"

"The court cannot help?"

"I'm afraid not, Miss Aliquot. Hearsay falls short of empowering subpoena. Do you understand?"

"Yes, your honor. I will do my best."

"I thank you, Miss Aliquot. God speed."

191

Jeanne Marie got back to Congo Square in the late afternoon, soaked with sweat, her feet blistered from the tightness of her shoes, the thinness of the soles. The guardhouse was shut down and secured with a large padlock. Still, she gave it a wide berth and entered Congo Square by the gate furthest from it. The music was getting louder at the center of the Square. She rested a moment and then walked painfully toward the Hitchins shelter.

At first she thought she was lost — she could find no trace of the shelter. She went back and forth, taking her bearings by her remembered sightings of the guardhouse. Finally, she stood where the front door of the shelter had been and, feeling certain she was in the right place, raised a prayer to St. Anthony.

An old man with a gnarled cane as bent as he was came limping toward her. He wore a loin cloth, the remnants of a straw hat, and a slightly exasperated expression. "Gone," he said, waving his cane. "Gone way away."

"Do you know where?"

"No. Just gone."

Jeanne Marie thanked him as he turned to go. She stood there for a time, feeling a deep sorrow, an awful desolation. My God, she thought, is that all there is? Dear little Essie forever gone? Unanointed, unshriven, eaten by dogs? Can it be, dear Lord? Can it be?

And she sank slowly to the ground and began to weep, bitterly, uncontrollably.

The old man squatted in front of his hutch and looked on impassively, spitting at regular intervals.

❧ ETIENNE ❧

FIFTY-ONE

Wednesday

These days I am a much reduced man. I never knew how much Antoine meant to me until he was gone. His sharp raps at my door, his voice ebullient as he suggested dinner at the St. Charles, a night at the opera, or a piano concert by Louis Moreau Gottchalk. All of this is gone because I can't yet bear to do any of it without him. What a loss is there! What an emptiness!

And now my dear Henriette is ailing. It breaks my heart to see her at Mass, her beautiful face lusterless, her movements slow and stiff, only her eyes shining, still lighting up the parchment of her skin — the light within never fading, incandescent, growing more intense as she weakens.

She has had two serious falls in the past month. One was on the staircase at 72 Bayou Road, and the other at Mass at St. Mary's. She turned from the communion rail and simply collapsed. The nuns helped her to her feet. She was more embarrassed than injured, but she was in bed ten days before she was well enough to get around.

Why does God not take better care of his own? A stupid question, I know, but I ask it. She is surely very precious to him, yet he has allowed her to be beaten down, all but broken. I am convinced that she has attained a level of prayer that is very close to mystical union. I don't know how many times I have prayed with her over the torn body of some poor derelict or some dying slave, and I have seen her transported, rapt in prayer the intensity of which I can only imagine. At those times there was a purity, a holiness in the air that overcame the stink of the room — a scent like wild flowers, or rose petals. I swear this is true before my God, yet I never — at any of

193

those times — asked Henriette if she was aware of the aroma. I think I was afraid of the answer. "Why, of course," she would have said. "That is the Holy Ghost, come to fetch her soul."

Just so. She always talks to God as though he were physically present in the room, just as she talks to me! She even chides God at times. I've heard her say, bending over some poor wretch, "Her soul must be saved, dear God, because it is a beautiful soul. You created it, and now you must save it. It is the right thing to do. After all, she did not choose not to know you, any more than she chose to be a slave. Therefore, dear Father, let her approach your holy table, hold her to your warm breast, and reassure her of eternal life."

I am transcribing from notes I made immediately after a certain incident about three months ago. A woman was dying of seven bleeding cancers up and down her body, one as big as a saucer. And the stench in the room was almost beyond endurance. Yet there was Henriette bending over her, calling upon God in her tenderly strident way to do right by his poor, his suffering, his bloody dying meek! And when the scent of roses came into that room, I gasped, and I looked around, and I felt Christ himself standing between Henriette and me! I do not exaggerate, I do not dissemble, I do not lie! He was there and I almost swooned with the brilliance and terror of it!

The next morning I said Mass like a man possessed, a man being burned free of all his impurities by the holy flame of Henriette's love of God. It magnified my poor unworthy soul to an intensity of passion for the living Christ, his Sacred Heart, so that I was brought to ground! I fell on the sacristy floor literally unable to stand to the fervent fire and force of his love for men, of his love for Henriette!

I should now, as a prudent chronicler, retrench, say that I got carried away — imagination gone amok. That I will now be sensible and repudiate my excesses. But, by God, I tell you that I cannot! I tell the truth. And if you should say that it is clear that I love Henriette, why then so be it. I do love her, but it is not a carnal love. It is a love that, in her presence, exalts me — puts me in awful, nearly palpable touch with the face of the living God.

I will stop now. She is a saint, and I am not. And I must not mistake lovesickness — if that's what it is — for any kind of personal sanctity. I must learn to step back out of her light, to let her shine alone in this darkness, and not intrude my pernicious self into her colloquy with God. I have smelled the roses and I have seen the light, but it is not my light, and they are not my roses. I must tend to the hard business of saving my own immortal soul, if the gentle God will have me.

❧ HENRIETTE ❧

FIFTY TWO

Henriette wrote:

My heart rebels, wishing to leave my body and my soul for
their lack of charity, for their gross indifference to blatant
human suffering. My heart weeps, my soul shrivels at the
news. Poor Father Pinchot has been confined to one of the
isolation wards at Charity Hospital, until recently the city's
insane asylum. He had taken, poor man, to carrying a heavy
wooden cross up and down Bourbon Street, wearing his filthy
white habit, his sandals, and a crown of rose thorns, shouting
obscenities to one and all, telling them that Christ was coming
soon to remove the bowels of sinners and, having hollowed
them out, to cast them into hellfire with their genitals wrapped
around their necks.

I am loathe to write such things, but I heard them often
with my own ears. And I longed to go to him, to tell him
that Jesus loved him, that I loved him, that there was loving
salvation for him if only he would turn to it and embrace
it. Indeed, I tried once, and he scooped up several handfuls
of horsedung and threw them at me — tried to rub them in
my face — calling me the whore of Babylon, the seducer of
young girls!

Dear God! I faint to write of these things. Yet I cannot
do any less. For I feel that I might have done more for the
poor man. Had I intervened earlier, had I only stood to his
vituperation and smiled or bowed my head as he heaped it

196

upon me, I might have broken through to him, I might have given him pause, I might even have been the tiny rod of light and grace that might well have brought him up short. But I had too much pride, too much indignation, and, to say it plain, I walked away from him, time and time again!

May Jesus forgive me my weakness! May the Blessed Virgin Mary, exemplar of the peculiar strength and unflinching courage that God has given to women, forgive me. For I failed, failed my womanhood and failed my blessed Christ and his intrepid and holy mother! I feel this deeply. I will not allow its effect to diminish. I shall wear the scar and shame of it to my grave. God have mercy upon my cowardly soul!

Amen.

❧ ETIENNE ❦

FIFTY-THREE

Sunday

I am very concerned about Henriette. Ever since the confinement of Father Pinchot, she has been distressed, as if she is personally responsible. Nothing could be further from the truth. She endured his excesses and his ridiculous public displays with great patience and sympathy. The only thing she should have done was come to me earlier about the problem.

But she is, if possible, even more concerned about the war. She feels that we — the people of the southern states — have brought it upon ourselves. I couldn't agree with her more, but I cannot agree that we, the clergy, could have done more to bring slavery to an end. If we raised our voices, we were not listened to and often told to stay out of politics — as if the thing were really a political, not a moral issue. I might have said more, even to Antoine's dismay, but I truly had no idea that it would come to this so quickly.

But back to Henriette. She sees the war as God's judgment upon the South and is quite certain that the South will lose. And this — although she thinks it will be the just result — is what dismays her most acutely. This land is hers, New Orleans is hers, and she wants New Orleans to become one of God's shining cities. She even went so far as to tell me once that the Mardi Gras, with all its pagan and satanic trappings, could one day become a true parade of pre-Ash Wednesday penitence, the solemn and triumphant demonstration of the Church Militant willing to scourge and flail itself for the next forty days of Lent in the cause of the redemption of souls. I have never actually seen any of the Mardi Gras — usually I spent the day and the night in prayer before the altar at St. Augustine's. But from what

I've heard, you might as well have asked the Visigoths to turn right at the Rubicon and ride into the sea clad in sackcloth and ashes.

Yet my heart goes out to her utterly, for she so ardently wants the South and especially New Orleans to turn to God. "This," she told me not so long ago, "is where Christ weeps most sorrowfully. And this is where his church will live or die in the South. If New Orleans falls to the devil, then it will take a thousand years for his church to reinstate itself." She may well be right. The strong Catholic tradition here is simply that, a tradition, and I could count the truly devout nonclergy whom I know on three fingers.

Well, we are in the hands of God, ultimately, but I must say, very quietly, that while I trust in God, I am no longer sure that I trust him to do what I fully believe or expect him to do. He is taking the long view here, I'm afraid, and it well may be much longer than I have to live. But what can we do but persevere and pray that God will at last grant Henriette her South, her New Orleans, and her order of black nuns.

❧ HENRIETTE ❦

FIFTY-FOUR

Henriette heard the commotion as she came out of a side entrance of Charity Hospital. She walked toward the raucous sounds and screams with a familiar queasy feeling in her stomach. Another public outrage, another street drama. From the sounds of it, it was not a minor event.

The first thing she saw was a white man with a pistol standing in front of a small building under construction. He was saying to a policeman, "Don't give a damn! Ain't nobody goin' to tear up my new floorboards to fetch out no crazy nigger bitch.'

Across the street, seated against another building, was another white man holding his stomach. There was blood all around him on the bleached board sidewalk. A woman was bending over him, whom Henriette recognized as Marie Laveau.

There was a black woman screaming nearby, claiming that she was a voodoo queen and that she'd done nothing more than kill the "debbil white man," and that she was declaring her kingdom on earth.

Henriette crossed to Marie Laveau, who immediately straightened, smiled a small, sad smile.

"Henriette. I was about to baptize him. You must do it. He is near death."

She handed Henriette a small mustard bottle full of water, and Henriette immediately bent to the man. "I baptize thee in the name of the Father, and of the Son, and of the Holy Ghost. Amen."

The man looked up at her and his mouth moved, but no words could be heard. He died with eyes wide open, looking at her.

Henriette bent, took his wrist, and searched for a pulse. Then she reached up and brushed his eyes shut. She stood up and looked at Marie Laveau. "Thank you, Marie." She started to hand the bottle back, but Marie held up one hand.

"The woman. She is not one of mine."

"The screaming woman? Where is she?"

"In under the floor of the new building."

Henriette looked. The flooring was no more than a foot off the muddy ground. "My God. It doesn't seem possible."

"I was taking her to the hospital, to commit her to the insane ward. The man complained that her snake had struck at him, and she stabbed him several times."

"She has a knife?"

"And a snake. It is quite poisonous. I couldn't get it away from her." Marie held up one hand, which was streaked with blood. "She is very fast with the knife."

The woman screamed again, something about her soul and the Sacred Heart of Jesus and, "Get back, debbil! I'm holy!"

Henriette looked at Marie Laveau. "She doesn't sound like a non-Catholic."

"She is not mentally well."

"Still." Henriette said.

"Now, Henriette. Don't even think of it. She is extremely dangerous."

"She will listen to me, I think."

"She will kill you, Henriette."

"But I must take that chance. She may be dying already from snakebite."

Marie Laveau put her hands to her hips. "Henriette Delille! I cannot allow you to go in under those floorboards after a mad woman!"

Henriette spoke in a quiet, firm voice. "Don't try to stop me, Marie. An immortal soul hangs in the balance. God is with me."

Henriette turned and then looked back. "What is her name?"

"Malvina."

Henriette held up the bottle of water. "I will return this to you later, Marie."

"I don't want it! I don't want you to go in there! I see only disaster!"

Henriette smiled. "Then pray for me, Marie. God listens to every one."

Henriette did not hesitate. She walked around to the place closest to where the woman's screams could be heard. This happened to be where the new bar had just been installed. The clearance between ground and floorboards was perhaps twelve inches.

"Where the hell you think you're going?" said the owner, waving his revolver.

"I'm going to save a soul," Henriette said. She immediately got to her knees, ducked her head, and crawled in under the floorboards.

"Hey!" the owner shouted. "Come outta that! Hey, you police! You see what's she's doing?"

Henriette was now out of sight. The policeman had seen Henriette disappear and came over to the owner nonchalantly. "You want the first one out of there, don't you?"

"Well, yeah I do. But now I got two."

"No. You got the only lady in New Orleans with the guts to bring her out and save your goddamn floorboards."

Henriette's dress was caught almost immediately on the rough lumber of the flooring's underside. She pulled the cloth free, tearing it in the process, and eased slowly in the hot dark toward where Malvina was still shouting imprecations in the far corner. "Dear Jesus," she prayed, "give me the courage." Henriette had always been a claustrophobe, had always dreaded tight places, especially those that constricted her simplest movements. She was now almost entirely constricted. She didn't try to turn back, and she knew that she could not. She could only go forward and hope that the clearance between floorboards and earth would somehow increase.

"Don't you come near me, you debbil! I see yous! You come near me, I give you the knife! God's truth!"

When she was almost to Malvina, Henriette saw the snake. It was coiled near Malvina's feet, and was poised to strike. Henriette stopped crawling and called to Malvina. "Are you all right?"

"I'se powerful in the Lord and the debbil, woman! Don't you come on!"

But Malvina's voice was fading, fairly sharply now. "Have you been bitten by the snake?"

"Oh, yes. Many, many times. He don't like it under this here. But he my protector and my charm. He don't mean me no evil. But he bite you. Oh, yes, he bite you."

Henriette gathered herself, easing forward. Malvina's voice was fading. She was clearly dying, and, as Henriette got within six or seven feet of her, she could see — in the sunlight slanting through the floorboards — that Malvina's face and breast were grossly swollen, and the snakebite wounds were oozing blood. A dozen snakebite wounds, at least, all of them perfectly discernible on her golden brown skin. "Have you ever been baptized?" Henriette said.

"Oh yes, woman. I's a voodoo queen. I gwine straight up."

"I mean in Jesus Christ. Have you ever been baptized?"

"Don't you come near me with that, you hear? What's that you got?"

"It's just plain water, Malvina. But it will wash you in the blood of the lamb."

"Snake! Bite her in the mouff! Y'hear? Bite her in the mouff!"

Henriette looked to the snake. It hadn't moved. Henriette eased forward, almost imperceptibly. The snake watched her, cold-eyed. The clearance between floorboards and earth had increased to perhaps seventeen or eighteen inches. Room enough to pour the water on Malvina's swollen forehead. Henriette inched closer and closer and was within about four feet when Malvina struck out with the knife. The tip of the blade swept across Henriette's forehead, and the rush of blood was almost immediate, filling Henriette's eyes. But Henriette surged forward, opened the mustard bottle, poured the water on Malvina's head, saying, "I baptize thee in the name of Father, Son, and Holy Ghost, amen."

"Whore!" Malvina screamed. "I kill you! I cut you!" Henriette felt the knife strike twice more as she pulled away. And then the snake struck, once, twice, both times in Henriette's left arm. She swooned and felt herself begin to fail. But then she felt something grasp her right ankle — something strong of grip and will and as she began to be pulled backward, she thought of the Archangel Michael and lost consciousness.

FIFTY-FIVE

It was Marie Laveau who had pulled Henriette from under the plank floor. She had watched as several men argued with the owner about prying up the floorboards. They disarmed him and started dismantling the bar. Marie Laveau watched a moment, saw that it would take much too long, and went in after Henriette. Malvina was already dead, but Marie pulled her out anyway, and both women were carried over to the hospital.

Henriette's snake wounds were superficial. They had struck on one of the rolled cardboard cuffs that Henriette had taken to wearing to keep her clothing out of open wounds. The knife wounds were more serious, but Henriette was able to walk out of the hospital on Marie Laveau's arm. They watched as Malvina's body was put aboard the hospital's flatboard hearse and then went over to Marie Laveau's house to mop Henriette's cuts and drink some strong tea. Henriette was clearly shaken but would have followed Malvina's body to the grave had Marie not prevented her.

"You must rest, my dear Henriette. That's enough heroism for one day."

"But I might at least pray at her grave."

"The hospital chaplain will see to that."

"Yes, of course. They have a chaplain."

"Don't you?"

"Well, we did have Father Pinchot. But he is suffering from an emotional distress. In fact, I was at the hospital to visit him, but it will have to wait. He is still not stable enough to receive visitors."

"Dear Henriette, God must love you very much. He heaps so much upon you."

Henriette looked at her closely. "That is a very deep insight, Marie."

Marie was smiling. "Not if you understand the divine comedy," she said. "And *you* are living it."

Over very strong black tea, Marie tended to Henriette's wounds, and the ladies discussed the state of the city and the state of the war. Marie had thoughtfully locked up her ceremonial snake and guided Henriette into a sitting room well away from the room given over to her altar. The house smelled sweetly of incense and of fresh flowers that were everywhere. Marie lived simply but well and wore her exotic identity as a voodoo queen with utmost modesty and grace.

"Are you comfortable, my dear?" she asked Henriette.

"Perfectly."

"I'll put an herb poultice on those knife wounds before you go. They will prevent any infection."

"Thank you, Marie. You are too kind. And thank you, again, for your bravery. I don't think I could ever have backed out from under that decking."

"Oh, God would never have let you die. Any more than he did Job on his dunghill."

"God is merciful."

"That's not exactly what I meant, but it will serve."

"And what do you think of this war, Marie," Henriette said, sensing it was time to change the subject. "Are we to be overrun and conquered?"

"This war is a two-edged sword. It may free the slaves, but it will destroy the South."

"The South will lose?"

"Contrary to gossip, I have no crystal ball," Marie said. "I cannot read the future. But, in my opinion, we lost the war the day we fired on Fort Sumter."

"And why is this?"

"Because, compared to the North, we have no factories. What we have is cotton fields. Acres of cotton fields."

"You are a wise woman, Marie."

"No. It is clear that Mr. Lincoln will see to it that the slaves are freed. And then...." She shook her head. "And then there will be chaos."

"And the poor church."

"Oh, the church will survive. You'll see to that, Henriette."

"You flatter me, Marie."

"Do I? Who else is there? You and your order of nuns. You will be the bedrock. This I confidently predict."

"An order? You do see an order of black nuns?"

"I see it in your eyes, Henriette. I see it in your indomitable soul. They call me a seer, and I see very well."

Henriette took her leave fondly, pleased that she had renewed her friendship with Marie Laveau. Though a bit unsteady on her feet, she walked to Potter's Field, found Malvina's new grave, and prayed over it. Then she walked back to the house on Bayou Road, full of the force of God. There would be an order of black nuns, an official order of the church, and she took it as only slightly untoward that it was a voodoo queen who had brought her to believe in it with absolute conviction.

❧ ETIENNE ❧

FIFTY-SIX

Tuesday

I have written today a letter to the Congregation of Religious in Rome to the effect that I thought it was high time that an order of black (nonwhite) nuns be taken under very serious consideration. I did not say, as I have before, that this had anything to do with the refusal of the white orders of religious women to consider the admission of black women. Rather I referred to the American war, to the imminent freeing of the slaves by President Lincoln, and to the fact that black nuns would be infinitely more effective in reaching and teaching and training black men and women than would the white orders.

It is not a proposition without flaw. The white orders will, of course, be just as vigorous as always in reaching out to the black community. But it is an argument I couldn't resist making — a peculiarly American argument — that just might catch the attention of the good cardinal in charge, if, indeed, a replacement for the newly deceased cardinal has yet been appointed.

I have decided not to mention this to Henriette. She has had quite enough of her hopes and expectations dashed already without my raising new ones.

The appointment of a new bishop still hangs fire. Pray God that the fire doesn't strike me.

⊰ HENRIETTE ⊱

FIFTY-SEVEN

Despite the ministrations of the Sisters of Charity and Marie Laveau, Henriette's knife wounds became infected and stubbornly refused to heal. The one on her forehead yielded first to treatment, but the ones across her left shoulder and arm would not go away. She did not allow the wounds to slow her down, however. She simply drained them of pus every night, bound them up, and pressed on the next day. But this pressing on, this pressing into the pain, did take its toll, and she began to tire quickly and to flag noticeably as the long days wore on.

Juliette was the one who finally took her to task. "You are not yourself, Henriette. Something is sapping you of strength, and I think it must be those knife wounds you refuse to show us."

"Oh, they're coming on very well, thank you, Juliette. I think they are almost healed."

"Then you won't mind letting us have a look."

"Please," said Josephine. "We are truly worried. You fainted today at Potter's Field."

"It was the heat. Nothing more."

"Then show us," Juliette said.

Gradually, Juliette and Josephine coaxed her out of her upper garments and then stood away dismayed.

"Dear Lord!" Juliette said. "Your shoulder, your arm! They are putrefied! Full of pus!"

"Oh, Henriette," Josephine said. And your left side! How could you even raise your arm?"

"Well, I cannot very well let them amputate. I must have my left arm. And if I continue treating it with a bit of laudanum —"

"You are going to Charity Hospital. Right now," Juliette said. "This very minute!"

"No, please. They will amputate. That's all they know how to do."

"Nonsense," Juliette said. "We will be right beside you. We will oversee them. The whole thing must be drained, and a wick put in, and it must be given a complete antiseptic bath. Josephine, fetch Charles and the wagon."

"Can't we treat it right here?"

"We might if this were a simple knife wound, but that woman must have poisoned the blade. Or perhaps the snake. I don't know, but we are going to the hospital, Henriette, and that is that."

Dr. Warren Stone, a renowned physician, happened to be leaving the hospital as Henriette was being brought in, and he recognized her from several encounters in clinics and other hospitals throughout the city. He stopped in front of the three women and addressed Juliette. "Is this not Henriette Delille?"

"Yes."

"She is ill?"

"She has a terrible infection. From knife wounds."

"Good Lord. We must have a stretcher." He turned to one of the Sisters of Charity. "Nurse? Sister? A stretcher here, if you please."

Dr. Stone operated that night. Famous for his work in arterial and vascular surgery, he had also led the movement for the use of anesthesia. Over her protests, he anesthetized Henriette, and proceeded to save her left arm and probably her life. It was a long operation that left both patient and doctor exhausted. But the doctor was ebullient afterwards. "It is not often one gets the opportunity to save the life of a living saint," he said.

FIFTY-EIGHT

Before she left the hospital some four days later, Henriette went to visit Father Pinchot. Her left arm in a sling, her face drawn and pale, her energy severely drained, she refused to be dissuaded from one last attempt to talk to the priest, to try to reach him in the place of despair to which he had retreated.

As soon as the door to his isolation cell was opened, he withdrew to the darkest corner, sat himself down back against the wall, and began to mutter the prayer of absolution.

Henriette, standing by the open door with two orderlies behind her, spoke softly. "Father Pinchot? May I speak to you?"

Silence. Then, "You are much reduced, Miss Delille. I feel none of your venomous power. Your judgmental zeal."

"I have suffered an accident. But I have come to seek your forgiveness." A pause. "I was very harsh to you, I'm afraid. I showed little mercy."

"Well." A long sigh. "Perhaps there is hope for you after all."

"You seem better yourself."

"No. No change. I am still God's last witness to the final depravity of the world. The awful sacrilegious depravity that will bring it to an end."

"You see no hope."

"None."

"I am sorry to hear you speak like this, Father. Jesus brought us salvation."

"Salvation to those who would embrace it."

"I embrace it."

"You do not embrace it. You turn it into a death masque. And you have gone too far. You are already dead, and you do not know

211

it. You put other people in their graves so that you can avoid getting into your own."

"Surely, you don't believe this, Father."

"Of course I do. With all my heart. The dead burying the dead is one of the final signs. You should know this. The dead know it. They know you belong to them."

"I baptize them. I give them another life. An eternal life."

Father Pinchot laughed bitterly. "You give them a hole in the ground. That's all. There is no other life. There is only a hole in the ground."

"But you spoke of salvation."

"It is the fashionable thing to speak of. The truth is, none will wholeheartedly embrace it. Therefore it doesn't exist. You know Descartes? 'I think therefore I am'? But the obverse is just as true. I do not think, therefore I am not. I believe, therefore I am. I do not believe, therefore I am not. And we do not believe. Therefore we are dead, unsalvageable."

"Father, those are all just words."

"Yes, and the Word, he was just a word."

"Father, you blaspheme."

"One has to, to tell the truth. And the truth is you are dead, and you will remain dead, because you do not truly believe. Among other things."

Then he began to laugh, bitterly, with a dreadful, hacking punctuation. "Father Pinchot, please!" Henriette cried. "God loves you!"

"God loves God, you ignorant peasant! Go now, find your grave and get into it! You are the walking dead, and you offend me!"

Henriette, with tears running down her face, wrote:

I believe in God, I hope in God. I love. I wish to live and die for God.

She paused, her tears staining the page. Then she wrote again.

I believe in God, I hope in God. I love. I wish to live and die for God.

Before she slept, she had written her prayer thirty-seven times, the last three times — having run out of ink — using blood from her draining wound.

FIFTY-NINE

Sometime later Henriette was brought back to Bayou Road on Charles's buckboard. She had collapsed at the Holy Family infirmary after baptizing a slave girl wounded in a gun fight who kept saying that she believed in the devil. "That's all right," Henriette had said. "So do I." She had finished the baptism just as Father Rousselon came through the door. She said, "Thank God" and then fell forward into Father Rousselon's arms, saying, "last rites."

The women carried her up to her room, put her to bed, and started a round-the-clock vigil. The doctor who attended the women repeated his diagnosis of utter exhaustion and recommended complete rest. "We'll have to tie her down," Juliette muttered, but, in fact, Henriette was too sick to move.

She had purchased a tomb at St. Louis Cemetery No. 2 several months before and had engaged a Mr. B. Fernandez to do the necessary concrete work. She asked to see Fernandez and went over with him what would be written on her tombstone. She was determined to have everything in order when she died, so that her passing would not be a problem to anyone.

On the morning of November 16, 1862, after Father Rousselon had given her Communion, she asked that he stay on for a moment. He sat down by the bed and said, "you are looking a little better."

213

Josephine, who had remained in the room for propriety's sake, added, "You've finally got some color in your face."

Henriette shook her head. "We have all seen this," she said. "It is the last flush of health and lucidity that God in his mercy gives to us just before the end."

"You are sure of this?"

"Yes, dear Father. I will go within the hour."

"Henriette, do not do that!" said Josephine. "Don't make up your mind that you are going, or you will. I know you too well!"

"Dear Josephine, my will has nothing to do with it. God wills my death, and I embrace it."

"But do not be so eager!" Josephine said.

"Oh, why not, dear Josephine? It is the grail we yearned for, from the time we were little girls. Now it is within my grasp."

"You are not afraid?"

"No, dear Father. I am sure of my welcome."

"So am I."

"But the order," said Josephine. "We need you to bring it all about."

"And you will have me. In heaven. Praying that you will complete what we have started. God intends that others finish the task, but I will be with you every moment." Her eyes become suddenly duller, and she reached for Father Rousselon's hand. "Dear Father, you have been so good to us. You have made it all possible. Now you must persevere, just a little bit longer. You must keep them together and keep their eyes on the vision. We will be a duly constituted religious order, and you will see to it. You will promise me that?"

"With all my heart."

"I am going now, but I will be with you always, in the heat of the day and the watches of the night. Speak to me and I will hear you, and I will press our cause before the throne of God. You will never be alone. This I swear to you, and God assures it."

Father Rousselon leaned down to her. "I will speak to you, dear Henriette, in all of my Masses and in every waking moment."

"I know you will, dear Father," she said, her voice failing to a whisper. "I have leaned upon your kindness, I have depended upon your charity, I have counted upon your holiness and compassion. Now, at the end, I call upon your blessing, the entire power of your priesthood, to see me through to the divine presence, to the glorious shining face of God. I will sleep tonight in the arms of Our Lord and Savior Jesus Christ. Come soon, dear Father Rousselon. I will miss you."

She died, and as he got to his feet, Etienne was not at all surprised as the scent of roses filled the room.

The authorities attributed Henriette's death to tuberculosis.

❧ ETIENNE ❦

SIXTY

Thursday

I climbed to the pulpit at St. Augustine's like a man climbing a gallows, so broken that I almost hoped there would be a noose waiting for me at the top.

I had been up all night and hadn't written a word of my eulogy. But I had long ago memorized my text, and that at least got me started.

"In the Song of Solomon we read, 'I am black, but comely, O ye daughters of Jerusalem, as the tents of Kadar, as the curtains of Solomon. Look not upon me because I am black, because the sun hath looked upon me; my mother's children were angry with me; they made me keeper of the vineyards.'

"Today, dear sisters and friends, we bury a saint. She was black, and she was comely, and a more zealous keeper of the Lord's vineyards never lived. She spent herself in his employ so unstintingly, so fiercely, so humbly that she is justly known as a servant of slaves.

"We who knew her watched her comings and goings, day and night. We saw her rescue and bring home the most pitifully wretched of this city. She would wash their bodies, and tend to their wounds, and speak to their souls. And, in the process, she broke herself upon the holy rack of divine compassion. She didn't see Jesus as we see him. We see him as through a glass darkly. She saw him clearly. And she welcomed her Lord Christ to the bedside of a dying slave as a dear friend come to celebrate with her the salvation of yet another soul.

"When I look upon a crucifix — Christ nailed agonizingly to a rough-hewn crosstree — I think of the incredible pain he suffered,

and I thank him, and bless myself, and move on. Henriette Delille
did not move on. She stayed with him for all of her fifty years. She
fashioned her own cross, put herself upon it, and took on the pain.
She had chosen her moment in time, and she held it fixed in the
forefront of her vision until the agony and suffering and despair
of the crucified Jesus was hers…the raising of the hammer, the
passage of the nails, and the flash of his sacred blood.

"Often I have been with her, anointing a dying slave, and have
become aware that she was seized by a different reality. I was anointing a slave, but *she* — she was washing the body of Christ, dressing
his wounds, stanching the flow of his blood, assuring him of his
Father's love.

"She is with him now, her Beloved, and only that thought makes
this ceremony endurable. I salute you, Henriette Delille, even as I
mourn your loss. And I will say my goodbye to you in the words of
a poem written for another crusader:

> Soldier of Christ, well done,
> Rest from thy Love's employ.
> The battle's fought,
> The victory won.
> Enter Thy Master's joy."

Epilogue

Worn out by the work, on November 17, 1862, Henriette Delille died at the age of fifty years old while a community of twelve nuns in prayer were again asking God to spare her life. The people who gathered at her funeral, free people of color, aristocratic white ladies, the poor, the aged, the orphans, and most of all, her friends, the slaves, all testified "by their sorrow" how keenly felt was the loss of her who for the love of Jesus Christ made herself the humble and devoted servant of the slaves.

— Sister Audrey Marie Detiege
Henriette Delille: Free Woman of Color

Postscripts

Father Etienne Rousselon died on June 15, 1866. He was returning from a trip to France and fell into the open hatchway of his ship shortly after it had docked in New York. He was sixty-six years old.

After Henriette Delille's death and the loss of her leadership, the Holy Family community almost came apart. Four or five of the latest newcomers left immediately. Three more left somewhat later. The community survived this crisis, and by 1900 the Holy Family Sisters had a motherhouse and novitiate, eight schools, orphanages, and homes for the elderly in New Orleans. They staffed convent schools in Opelousas, Baton Rouge, and Donaldsonville, Louisiana. Today the Sisters of the Holy Family are the largest community of religious women in Louisiana.

On July 27, 1881, the community purchased the property at 717 Orleans, just behind the cathedral. It had been the site of quadroon balls for years. The sisters turned the ballroom into a dormitory for young lady boarders and orphans.

Approximately six weeks after Henriette Delille's death, President Lincoln, on January 1, 1863, signed the Emancipation Proclamation.

The cause for canonization of Henriette Delille was introduced in 1989. The Vatican reviewed what was presented at the time and gave permission to the Sisters to go on to an official biography and to a closer study of her life and her virtue. The Cause is still pending and entirely viable. If and when she is canonized, she will be the first African-American woman so honored in the history of the American Catholic Church.

Prayer to
Mother Henriette Delille

Dear Heavenly Father, in view of the sacrifice of Jesus Christ, our Lord, and through the intercession of Mother Henriette Delille, we pray that this particular intention be granted. [Name it.]

Mother Henriette Delille, inspired by your example of faith in God, prayer, joyful sacrifice, and loving concern for others, especially the poor, the needy, and the most abject of society, we implore your help in this our need. We place our petition before you and earnestly request that you intercede for us with our heavenly Father that our prayer be granted. Mother Henriette Delille, pray for us.

Nihil obstat:
> Franz Graef, Censor Librorum
> New Orleans, December 6, 1989

Imprimatur:
> Most Reverend Francis B. Schulte
> Archbishop of New Orleans, December 6, 1989

ABOUT THE AUTHOR

William Kelley (1929–2003) was a professional writer with screenplays, TV series, pilots, and novels to his credit. He won an Academy Award for co-writing the Best Original Screenplay for *Witness* in 1986. He had over 150 television credits for series, movies, and pilots. Some of his television writing and co-producing projects included *The Winds of Kitty Hawk* (Movie of the Week), *The Demon Murder Case* (Movie of the Week), and episodes of *Gun-smoke, Kung Fu, How the West Was Won, Serpico, Petrocelli, Dukes of Hazzard, Judd for the Defense*, as well as many others. In addition to the Oscar, Bill also won two Golden Spur awards for Best Western Scripts. Through the years he authored five novels: *Gemini, The God Hunters, The Tyree Legend, Witness*, and *The Sweet Summer*.

Mr. Kelley taught screenwriting and lectured at numerous universities. He lived with his wife, Nina (1932–2010), a renowned California landscape painter, in the foothills of the Sierra Nevada in northern California.

www.ingramcontent.com/pod-product-compliance
Lightning Source LLC
Chambersburg PA
CBHW011406010726
47495CB00009B/2792